PENGUIN BOOKS

THE VIADUCT

David Wheldon was born in Ashby de la Zouch, Leicestershire, in 1950. He was educated at Sidcot School and at Bristol University, where he read Medicine. He now lives and works in Bedford.

With *The Viaduct* David Wheldon won the Triple First Award for 1983. This award was instituted in 1982 by The Bodley Head, Penguin Books and Book Club Associates, with the intention of encouraging young authors and widening the market potential for the first novel. *The Viaduct* was chosen from among 641 typescripts submitted for the prize and was the final choice of the two consultant judges, Graham Greene and William Trevor.

DAVID WHELDON

——

THE VIADUCT

PENGUIN BOOKS

Penguin Books Ltd, Harmondsworth, Middlesex, England
Penguin Books, 40 West 23rd Street, New York, New York 10010, U.S.A.
Penguin Books Australia Ltd, Ringwood, Victoria, Australia
Penguin Books Canada Ltd, 2801 John Street, Markham, Ontario, Canada L3R 1B4
Penguin Books (N.Z.) Ltd, 182–190 Wairau Road, Auckland 10, New Zealand

First published by The Bodley Head Ltd 1983
Published in Penguin Books 1984

Copyright © David Wheldon, 1983
All rights reserved

Made and printed in Great Britain by
Richard Clay (The Chaucer Press) Ltd,
Bungay, Suffolk
Set in Linotron Ehrhardt

I

The viaduct had been constructed by the Eastern Provincial Railway and ran from one green hill to another with eight great arches supported by slender brick piers. It was very high; so high that under certain atmospheric conditions the railway it supported was invisible in low cloud, and only the rising piers were visible. The city lay beneath the viaduct, and the viaduct dwarfed the buildings, even the cathedral with its tapering spire and the city hall with its green copper cupola. Why permission had been given to build the viaduct was a mystery, unless in the last century the city had been so gripped with the prestige of being a railway terminus that it had allowed the Eastern Provincial Railway Company to erect that formidable structure. Perhaps the citizens, at the conception of the railway, had been quite unaware of the massive scale of the viaduct which now transected their city.

The railway that ran over the viaduct had never been a financial success, and was now derelict.

The viaduct was completely redundant, but still it dominated the city. The permanent way between its parapets had long since been taken over by nature; grasses and small trees had taken root and had to some extent made the viaduct a natural part of the landscape, as though it had been made not by man but by some freakish upheaval of the earth.

A man stood on the viaduct. He was equipped for walking, for he wore heavy boots, tough canvas trousers and jacket, and on his back he carried a pack. He stood silently, ignoring the wind which, strong at this high altitude, sang in the fretted copings of the viaduct's parapets. He stood looking ahead of him, his gaze fixed on the vanishing perspective of the overgrown railway line. He tried to ignore the city beneath him, a difficult thing to do, for the day was a Sunday, and the time a quarter to eleven, and the foreshortened towers and spires of the city churches were banging their bells, one church competing with another until the sound that reached the top of the viaduct had become a steady but confused metallic clangour. The only bell which, by virtue of its deep sonority, achieved any kind of individuality in that sea of sound was the tenor bell of the cathedral tower.

The man on the viaduct was oblivious to the sound, but stood, silently, staring ahead of him. Then spurred on by some inner drive he began walking, picking his way amongst the trees and shrubs that grew on the uneven path between the two parapets.

Halfway along the viaduct he met a man walking a dog. The dog, a black labrador, was little more than an active puppy, and strained at its lead.

It was inevitable that the two men would meet. For a moment it seemed that they would pass each other without speaking. They looked at each other without any greeting, without any recognition. It was only when

(6)

the man with the dog had passed that the other called to him.

"Excuse me."

The man with the dog turned, pulling at the dog's lead. "Sit, Solomon!" The dog ignored his command. "Sit, you black beast." He smiled at the man and nodded in the direction of the dog. "He's only nine months old."

The other man saw all this with his grave brown eyes. "When did the railway close? I went to the terminus to get a train."

The man with the dog began to laugh; he shook his head in a perplexed manner. "When did it close?" He gestured to the trees that sprang from the railway bed. "Ten years ago, I suppose. Are you a stranger here?"

"No, this is my city. I was born here."

"Are you having me on?" The man with the dog might have thought he was talking to a madman to judge by his expression. "Where have you been all this time?"

The other man sat on the edge of the parapet, apparently unaware of the terrifying drop on the other side. "You can guess the answer to that, I suppose."

And the man with dog saw the close prison haircut, the thinness, the wariness of the eyes.

The two men watched the dog. The owner of the animal, tired of continually restraining him, leaned down and unclipped the lead from the collar. The dog, released, bounded away along the viaduct until he came to a clump of stunted bushes.

"There are rabbits up here," said the man who owned the dog.

"That's strange." The man who sat on the parapet stood, and looked down at the city below him. The sight of the foreshortened city did not appear to disturb him; in another man the sight might have brought about an acute vertigo. "It seems strange to think of rabbits up here, above the city. And the trees, and this overgrown wilderness." He turned to the other man. "It's a constitutional walk of yours, this viaduct?"

"No, it isn't. I've never been up here before. I live down there –" He pointed to an anonymous clutch of terraced houses, not far from the spire of a church whose weathercock revolved endlessly in the complex eddies of wind that swept through the arches of the viaduct. "I've never looked down at my home from up here."

"You've not been up here before, then?"

"Never. Except, of course, on the train, when I was younger; I remember that you couldn't see anything of the city from the train windows." He joined the released prisoner, and they both leaned on the coping of the parapet. "It doesn't seem safe up here, now. I don't know how much maintenance they do."

The freed man laughed, briefly and involuntarily. "You're as safe up here as down there, I suppose. It would be all the same if the thing fell."

"I don't mean that. It's the height here. The height of it. The fact that the city is so small; why, if you threw a stone from here you could hit the roof of any one of a

(8)

dozen churches." He paused. "I never realised there were so many churches in the city."

The freed man turned his back on the prospect and resumed his seat on the parapet. "I daresay you can see my home from here."

"Where did you live?"

"I meant the prison. You can see it from here. I could point out the very block I was in. The window faced the viaduct, here, and that was all I could see. The stonework of it; the arches. The way that the sun caught the stonework. I used to look out, up here, and I knew that the first thing I would do would be to travel along that viaduct, away from the city. I'm known here. I can't stay here." There was something strained about his voice. "It's good of you to listen to me. Not many would."

"It's nothing to me." The owner of the dog looked along the perspective of the railway. "Solomon!"

"You see, the viaduct was the only thing I could see. When they let me out the first thing I did was to go to the terminus, to catch a train, to get away from the city, to get away from it all. I couldn't stay here." He felt in his pocket for a pipe, and brought out a small briar with an aluminium stem that must have been bought very recently, for the bowl was shiny and new, and the mouthpiece unstained. "I wonder if all families are as proud and as condemnatory. Me? They'd never speak to me. I must get away. I can't live here." He lit his pipe and coughed, looking down at the glowing bowl of the pipe. "It'll take me some time to get used to it again." He put the pipe back in his pocket. "It seems so bloody strange that this thing we're standing on, this viaduct, means nothing now. I tell you it meant so much to me, back there, when it was all I had to look at."

"So you aren't going anywhere in particular."

"I'm getting out of the city. I'm halfway there now." He gave another of his preoccupied laughs, as if he knew that he was speaking half to himself. "Up here I'm as far away from it all as I could ever be."

"Where would you have gone?"

The freed man shrugged his shoulders. "I never thought of that." He was aware of the other man's gaze, and the fact shook him out of his introspection. "I suppose you want to know why I was in there."

"I never asked the question."

"No, but you wanted to."

"Well, I must go." He smiled with a forced geniality. "That dog of mine. He's no more than a pup." He looked at the clump of bushes. "Solomon! Come out of there, you black pig."

The freed man stood up. "Where does this track go?"

"Come here, Solomon." The dog's owner whistled, and the animal bounded out of the bushes, its tongue lolling. The animal's eyes were mischievous and bright. Its owner rattled the chain of the lead. "Come here." He glanced at the other man. "What did you say?"

"Where does this track go to?"

"I don't know. I'm no traveller. I've had no reason to take the railway since I was a child. I don't know." He chained the dog, and looked at the city.

"I shall have to find that out for myself, then." The freed man began to walk down the track. He did not look back at the owner of the dog, and he did not look down at the city.

Down below the noise of the bells had stopped, and the city was silent with a Sunday silence.

*

In the city beneath the viaduct the towers were silent. Midday had progressed through a hot afternoon to a dusty evening; the shadows stretched across the roofs of the churches and the houses and the municipal buildings, across the red pantiled roofs of the poor quarter, across the turreted roofs of the bishop's palace. In a few more hours those shadows would lengthen until they fled across the river valley and the water-meadows. In half an hour's time the city bells would ring. Now the bells were silent.

A woman sat in a small quadrangle where the sun penetrated. This courtyard, measuring no more than twenty feet in any dimension, was the private yard of the house in which she lived. It was overlooked by no windows other than her own, and these windows were open to allow the fresh air of the hot summer into the house. The woman sat on a windsor chair at a small table; both these articles of furniture were clearly not intended for use out of doors; perhaps she had fetched them from her kitchen to take advantage of the summer air. The woman herself was tall and simply dressed. Her feet were bare. There was nothing on the table in front of her. She stared at the blank wall opposite her chair. Her face was expressionless, relaxed and neutral, as though she knew and appreciated the privacy of her courtyard.

Inside the house, through the open casements, the furniture could be seen obscurely, but a view of the interior of the house gave the impression that the woman who sat in the garden lived alone, was not given to entertaining, and had a sense of taste that might have been construed as being slightly outmoded; perhaps she was content to live in a house furnished by her parents, or her husband's parents. There was also an impression of order and security.

The two events happened at once. The shadow of one of the piers of the viaduct crept across the courtyard with a surprising rapidity, and with an equal rapidity the place grew cold. Coincidentally the doorbell rang.

The woman stood up. She looked about her, surprised that anyone should call at this hour. She smoothed her dress and, still bare-footed, she walked across her yard to the door. She made her way across the kitchen. The hall stretched ahead of her. She saw the silhouetted figures at the glazed front door. She pulled the door open.

"Yes, you know me," said the blunt-featured man who stood at the step. "You recognise me from the trial; I can see that." He had been staring into the woman's face; now he dismissed her, flapping the palm of his right hand impatiently, indicating that she was to get out of his way. "This is the house," he said, turning back to the two men who stood behind him. Again he addressed the woman. "Where is he?" He took a step into the house, and the woman retreated in front of him. "It'll save you time and agony if you tell me where he's hiding. Tell me which room, cupboard, wardrobe, roof, attic – but just tell me."

The woman retreated further into the hall. "What do you want?"

"Just tell me where he is." The man with the blunt features spoke with a simulated anger.

"He isn't here." There was nothing defiant in the woman's denial.

"I see. I'm supposed to believe that, am I? You forget that I saw you lie in the witness box, giving out lie after lie, to protect him."

"But why should you want him? He was released only today."

'I know that as well as you. There are fresh charges." He lit a cigarette. "I suppose you guessed that." Seeing that the woman did not answer he walked further into the house. "There are always fresh charges in these sedition cases."

He stood in the conservatory that led to the quiet courtyard. "This is your house?"

The woman nodded. "What do you want? Why are you here? What do you want?" The nervousness in her voice made her words difficult to distinguish. Her heart pounded in her chest.

"We can talk about it in the yard there." The man walked out into the courtyard. Each clematis flower glowed against the evenlit wall above the shadow.

In many ways there was something disturbingly familiar in the behaviour of that blunt-faced man. The way he took out his papers from his briefcase, and laid them on his table, making himself a desk. He sat down in the single chair in a most natural manner, as though he had been accustomed to sitting in that chair every fine evening of his life.

He sat down, and faced the woman. "You are cold?"

"No."

"Good." He rearranged his papers on the table, and brought out yet more official items from his case: a set of rubber stamps, a stamp pad, a stick of sealing wax, a dip pen and a bottle of ink. He turned to one of the other men. "Get her a chair. Then search the house. Leave us alone." He unbuttoned his jacket.

"You first met him when?" The man paused, the pen ready to dip into the ink bottle.

"You know this! I have told you all this at the trial!"

"Try and keep calm." The bored complacency had come back into the man's voice. "You met him when he was a casual labourer?"

"Yes."

"And you had sexual relations with him."

The woman started to cry; the man watched her, his attitude one of practised patience, as if he knew to a second when she would stop her weeping and speak.

"No, that wasn't the reason for it all," she said, her voice so indistinct that the man had difficulty in catching the words. He leaned forward over his desk. "You said that in such a horrible, cruel way."

"But you had sexual relations with him. He was

eighteen and you were thirty. You didn't seem worried by the fact then; you couldn't have been worried by the fact that the neighbours must have known about it. You newly widowed." He stood up, his face red and angry, but there was a calculated spuriousness in that anger. "Have you no shame? Have you no shame at all? Did you hold your husband's memory in so little regard that you went out and found the nearest labourer to your bed to satisfy you? If you were that kind of woman then, how can you have changed? Or do you think that you can soften me with your crying?" He paused. Although he frowned it was evident from his expression that he could just as well have smiled at the sight of the woman who stood in front of his desk.

Only a few seconds later and they sat in silence, the man observant and watchful, the woman now shuddering with tears. Around them the courtyard grew dark. Only the light from an upstairs window cast a stark square ray onto the flagged floor.

The man stood up, heavily. He walked over to the woman, and put an arm round her shoulder. "Very well then. Perhaps you were deceived by him. You can tell me; I want to know the truth." He bent down and patted her shoulder. "How did it happen?"

"Why do you want to know? You made a torment of his trial."

"The torment was of his own making." He paused. "Perhaps I was brutal just now, but I have my duty to think of, and sedition can be a terrible thing. The very fact that you were taken in by him shows that. I don't know. Perhaps you meant for the best. Do you think I have no understanding of how these things can happen? You are intelligent; I saw that at the trial, but, believe me, the intelligent are almost more gullible than the rest in these matters." He softened his voice. "Tell me how it happened."

"They were working out on the road, the three of them. It was a hot day." She stopped speaking.

"It was a hot day." The man, aware that his voice had been almost in mimic of hers, repeated the words in a soft solicitous undertone. "It was a hot day, yes, and you took them out some cider."

"No, not cider."

"Very well, it doesn't really matter what you took out to them."

"They were hot and thirsty, the three of them. Two of the men were older and obviously labourers – I remember the sight of their calloused hands as they took the glasses from me now, and the way their eyes looked at me."

"You invited them into this yard of yours?"

"Yes. It was hot on the road and there's no pavement, as you know, and the traffic was rumbling past, raising white dust."

"And the third of them? He was this man, I suppose?" The man took his arm from her shoulder. He drew in his breath. "You aren't telling me much, you know. You aren't telling me why he so attracted you."

"He was very silent."

"That's a very obvious thing to say," said the man with a heavy attempt at humour. "Is it a truism to say that women always find silent men attractive?"

"He was silent, and alone. It was clear that the other two did not want his company. They sat together, and talked between themselves. Alexander was quiet. Not aloof for the sake of aloofness, you understand."

"I think I understand."

"And he was so young and there was something in him that told me that he had some inner perplexity. I admit I watched him from the window. I saw that he had gone through some terrible experience, but he wouldn't relate it. I invited him into my house, and he stood there, in the front room, looking at the furnishings. It was a hot day, and he had no shirt. He was naked from the waist up. That fact embarrassed him, being in my front room without a shirt."

"You thought he was wounded, and you took compassion on him? Is that it?"

"He was wounded. I never guessed at the extent of his wounds until later. Until he knew he could confide in me."

"And you believed all that he said?"

The woman looked up. "Yes," she said, simply. "I had to believe him. It wasn't as though he was eager to spin me a tale; he never put himself forward. He was deferential. He was embarrassed. I wanted to help him. I think he was suspicious of me at first."

"And he moved in with you, here, and made you his mistress?"

The woman showed her first signs of anger. "Get out of my house. Get out of it, at once. And tell your men to get out."

The man laughed softly. "So he never came back when he was released this morning?"

"No, he never came back." The woman had walked to the door, her anger evaporating under the soft compliant questioning. "And, if you want to know, he refused to see me when I went up there on visiting days."

"He cast you off, did he?"

"Do you want to know the answer to that?"

"Your answer? Or the truth? Remember, I know you're a gullible woman. Always remember that."

"He refused to see me because he was ashamed. Proud and ashamed."

"Proud! A convict! A man facing fresh charges from the moment of his release!" The man laughed as though he himself had made an amusing joke.

Above their heads a window catch rattled.

The man stared up at the sound. "Tell me," he said, still looking up, "before I go," and there was a soft satisfaction in the tone of his voice, "did he do all his writing here?"

"He wrote at my husband's desk."

"I see."

"I read the things he had written. I had to read them to understand them."

"And you read the things that he had written and fell for his sedition, is that it?"

The woman opened the door to the house. "I gave him every encouragement. I believed in him."

"You believed in him. A seditioner. Were you in my position you would find that every seditioner has a fool who believes in him." He took a pace backwards, still looking up at the window. His voice was preoccupied. "It's sometimes difficult to distinguish between common criminality and the criminality due to some kind of perverse mental disorder. You must believe me when I say that."

The window was thrown open. A head peered down, hesitantly, as though waiting for instruction.

"What is it?" The blunt-faced man stared at the open window.

The voice of the man who leaned out of the window followed the question instantly. "We have found a box-file. There was a wardrobe in the attic bedroom. That wardrobe had a mahogany moulding; a sheet of plywood had obviously been recently nailed to it; we ripped the plywood away and found the box-file."

The blunt-featured man turned to the woman. "I take it that you knew it was there?"

"Yes, I did."

"There's a quiet defiance in your voice." He turned away and called up to the window. "What is in that file?"

"Typed pages. They're numbered."

The man who stood in the courtyard walked into the house. As an aside to the woman he said: "Next you'll be telling me that you typed his sedition."

He brushed past the woman, not speaking anything further to her. He walked into the front room, observing the narrow window, still unshuttered, the sideboard, the table, the writing desk. He saw the covered typewriter that lay on a shelf. "We can check the identity of type later." He looked up beyond the door to the stairs. "Bring down that file." He raised his voice. No longer was there need for any particular intonation; the command was a command.

He took the box in his hands, and opened it. He read a few lines of writing. He took out the mass of paper. As he did this he looked at the woman who stood in the doorway; for a moment it seemed that he was about to say something, for he opened his mouth. But no words were uttered; neither comment nor explanation was necessary.

His expression was not one of triumph; rather it was the expression of a man who had completed a task to his own satisfaction. And when the three men left the house, as though by coincidence the bells of the city churches and the great bells of the cathedral tower began to ring.

II

Even before *A.* had reached the end of the great viaduct that spanned the city he was aware of his pursuers.

He began to run, in the manner of a pursued man, although he was uncertain as to whether the figures behind him were in fact pursuing him. He reached the end of the viaduct, where the railway ran for a little way on flat ground before plunging into a deep cutting. He ran on, into the shadow of the cutting. The undergrowth hampered his running, and before he had gone far into the cutting he was forced to unstrap the pack from his back. He knew the worthlessness of the things it contained. For a few seconds he held the pack in his hands, and then he tossed it into a clump of bushes that grew beside the railway.

He ran light now.

He ran light, but he had nothing other than the clothes he wore and the few things in his pockets. He looked round and saw his pursuers. They seemed to be making no better progress than himself; if anything he had run faster than they, and now they were no more than small figures, intermittently seen between the spindly trees. He slowed his pace.

Had he imagined the pursuit? Were the three men

in chase of him? He looked back, and saw the three figures.

He was light, and they were heavily accoutred with their official uniforms. Once he saw the reflection of metallic light from one of the figures; perhaps the shining of a polished buckle. He saw no sign that they were armed.

Realising his advantage he stopped to catch his breath. He looked around him, at the dense undergrowth of the cutting. The light was dim and gloomy here, and the top of the cutting was forty or more feet above the track. The masonry of the sides of the cutting was lichened and slimy, and willow-herb grew in profusion. He looked ahead, and saw the growing denseness of the thin and spindly trees and the upward-striving plants. He must go on; there was no alternative. The sides of the cutting were unscalable. He plunged into the undergrowth; almost immediately he cut his right hand on something sharp. He looked down at his cut hand, and saw his own blood, dark red in the attenuated green light that filtered down through the foliage of the saplings.

He had torn his hand on a single strand of barbed wire that, covered by convolvulus, had been unnoticeable. He now saw that that wire stretched slackly across the track, stapled to a few leaning posts.

He climbed over the wire – looking down at it he saw that the barbs on it were long and frequent, as though the wire had been intended for a military and not an agricultural use – and fled further into the young forest of etiolated trees.

He stood in silence. Here, in this dank cutting, there was a sense of decay, for all the youthfulness of the thin trees that overarched him. The high walls of the cutting precluded any entry of light, and the sky was a band of blue above the reticulations of the leaves. He looked back. The three figures were nearer now, and, moreover, they were more in number. Men on horseback had joined his original pursuers. He heard the sound of distant horses' hooves even before he saw their riders. He knew then the certainty of pursuit, and he began to run, awkwardly, his footing uncertain in the mossy bed of the railway. Within a few yards he came to a choked stream; looking up he saw that a trickle of water fell from the stone facing of one side of the cutting. The sounds of insects were loud, and the sounds of the hoofbeats of his pursuers' horses were oddly muffled. The way ahead was, to his fearful mind, impenetrable. The sides of the cutting grew yet higher. He began to clamber over uneven ground; part of the cutting had caved in, and dressed stones lay ankle-deep in moss. The same thick moss covered the spindly trunks of the trees.

So anxious was he to escape that he did not see the man who stood by the bank of fallen stone until the latter called to him.

"You have no need to run. You've passed the boundary. They won't come any further."

A. looked at the man, distinguishing him with difficulty, for he was dressed in a suit of green corduroy that merged in with the decaying greenness of the moss and the trees and the lichen on the higher stones of the cutting. He was a tall man, thin, and he had his arms spread out, palms outermost, an expression perhaps intended to express an absence of weapon or the presence of good intention. "Didn't you hear me?"

A. was too exhausted to answer. He stood, panting like a dog, sweat shining on his face.

"You're all but done in," said the man in the torn corduroy suit. He did not move, though; he put his hands into his pockets. "You can run on, if you like, but it won't help you. They won't go past the boundary. I've seen this happen too many times to be mistaken about that."

"What boundary?" *A*. gasped the words almost voicelessly, but the standing man must have heard him.

"You saw the wire, didn't you?"

"I cut myself on it." *A*. held up his bleeding hand.

The standing man now cocked his head on one side and smiled. For the first time he moved, stepping with an easy caution down the terrace of fallen stones until he stood a few paces from *A*. "You're all but done. Your heart must be beating like a drum."

"The horses! I can hear the horses!" *A*. looked back along the track. "Where can I go?"

"I tell you that they won't come beyond their boundary." The man in green shrugged his shoulders. "You might as well believe me. It won't do you much good if you don't."

The sound of the horses was close now, and the cries of the pursuers were clear and distinct and strangely echoless in the dull confines of the cutting.

A., seeing that the only available way of escape lay beyond the standing figure of the man in the green suit, ran towards him and brushed past him. He touched his clothes as he passed, his head lowered, his feet uncertain on the treacherous ground. As he passed the man he heard him mutter.

"I've never seen such fear in a man." The man in the green suit stared at *A*. "Come back. Come back and look."

A., almost despite himself, turned and looked back. He saw the smile on the face of the tall man; he looked beyond.

The horsemen had stopped at the centre of the track, presumably at the barbed wire. One of them was dismounting. The sunlight glittered briefly on his brass helmet. The blue uniform and the braiding were very distinct.

The tall man had joined *A*., his strides long and lanky, his arms swinging by his sides. "I told you they would stop."

"What will they do now?"

"They'll stay there for a while. I've seen it before. They don't do much, except talk; they can't come any further."

"What's to stop them?"

The horsemen had by now seen *A*. One of them pointed. The faces all stared up as the hand pointed; one face was clearly distinguishable by its black moustache.

"I recognise that man," said *A*.

"I doubt it," said the other. "They all look much the same."

"No, I recognise him."

"I suppose he is a friend of yours?"

A. looked sharply at the tall man, who did nothing more than raise his eyebrows.

"So you say that you cut yourself on the boundary wire."

"Yes, not deeply."

"They say it's a good sign if you cut yourself on it. A local superstition. There are a lot of superstitions about the boundary wire, although it doesn't look much of a thing. I'm told that the horsemen have their own superstitions too. Perhaps that's why they won't cross the boundary. I don't know; that's only hearsay."

"How long will they stay there?"

"That depends on what you were, and why you fled them." The tall man took a closer look at *A*. "What's your name?"

He mentioned his name.

"That's a reasonable name. Fairly orthodox. Obviously you were not suffering for the crime of your family's name." He smiled, slowly. *A.* saw for the first time that his eyes were coloured more deeply around the rims of his irises than round the pupils; this unusual colouring gave a curiously fixed concentration to his gaze. "I suppose you could say I've helped you." Not waiting for a reply he went on, "And that might give me the right to ask why you were being pursued, and why you were so anxious to avoid capture."

"I was released today."

"That's obvious from your clothes. And they were trying to capture you again. That must mean that you have committed some political crime in the city; they never let those men go." He looked at A. with his concentrated gaze. "What did you do?"

"I wrote a book. I was foolish enough to try to have it published."

"Anonymously? The underground press?"

"No. I was open. I wanted to be truthful." A. was still looking at the horsemen who by now had all dismounted, and who were all staring at him silently. "I was foolish in those days."

"Perhaps not. Perhaps not. At least you were honest. I never respect anything that comes anonymously from the city." The tall man was now looking at the dismounted horsemen. "You hear so many garbled voices. What did you write about?"

"My life."

"You wrote about your life." He spoke with an easy tolerance. "And was there any crime there? What had you done that disturbed them?"

"My life was orthodox. My only crime was writing about it, and, I suppose, my attempt to publish it."

"What did they bring against you in your trial?" And then the tall man saw A.'s faintness. "Let us get away from here. You've had enough of it; I can see that. Besides, the horsemen, although they cannot cross the boundary, have a habit of staring. It's another of the local superstitions that their stare can make you faint. Have you ever noticed how fixed their stare is, as though they were drugged?" He did not wait for A. to answer, for the latter was near exhaustion. "It's a strange fact, that."

A., perhaps suggestible in his moment of sudden weariness, thought he saw some reason behind that particular superstition.

*

It should have been obvious that such a deep and steadily inclined cutting must lead to a tunnel.

The mouth of this tunnel, gaping its damp exhalations, had been furnished in the days of the Eastern Provincial Railway with a most impressive façade; about its rounded mouth were two masonry pilasters of great height. Indeed, the mouth itself had been impressively proportioned, far taller than the height of any locomotive or wagon that might once have passed through it. The proportion of the whole thing was spectacular, and now even in decay the arch of the tunnel and its stone surround had an impressive grandeur more suggestive of classical than of industrial architecture. The tunnel might have been an entrance to a tomb rather than a passage under a hill.

The very nature of the tunnel entrance showed the ambitions of the Company, for surely no mortal other than the permanent waymen could have seen it in full perspective during the working life of the railway. No railway passenger, travelling at speed, could have seen its fine proportions from a carriage window.

It was to this tunnel that the thin man in the corduroy suit led *A.* The pursued man's mind was still uneasy with the thought of pursuit, and with the thought of the single fixed stare of the horsemen who had halted at the boundary wire.

*

Two men had made their camp within the mouth of the tunnel. The floor was comparatively dry, but the moist wind that blew out of the tunnel portended an inner dampness. The light within the confines of the tunnel entrance was attenuated and green because of the foliage which fringed the stonework, and which now covered most of the entrance. The tall man in the green corduroy suit was one of these two men; he now stood at the mouth of the tunnel, looking down the cutting towards the viaduct, several miles away. He could make out, if only with great difficulty, the horsemen who still stood by the boundary fence. He knew that he could not be seen by them. He wondered what they were looking at, for they seemed to be staring, as one man, up to the side of the cutting.

His companion had stood by his side, slightly behind him, panting as though he had undergone some exertion. This newcomer was thin, like the first, but his thinness was less exaggerated because of his shortness. He wore a white shirt, more torn than dirty; that shirt had a ribbed front to it, and was collarless, as though it had once been a dress shirt. Over this he wore a leather jacket, longer than the usual pattern, a garment that came halfway down his thighs. He was carrying a bundle.

"What have you brought with you this time?" The tall man spoke, and stared at the other with his concentrated stare. "You are always bringing things in. You are a collector of rubbish. What is it this time?"

The small man laid the bundle down, and smiled subserviently. It was clear from the taller man's remark and the newcomer's smile that there could be no doubt as to who was leader and who was follower.

"I saw it all," said the man in the leather jacket. "I was out on the cutting when it happened. I saw your man there –" and he pointed to *A*. who, staring up from his stirring of a pot of stew which boiled on a portable paraffin stove, a task he had been told to do by the man who had first met him, looked at the newcomer. "I saw it all from the top of the cutting. I saw him walking along the track; I saw him begin to run, when he first knew he was being pursued. It was difficult to keep pace with him, for all that it's easier to run on the top of the cutting than it is on the track. I kept low while the horsemen passed." He looked down at *A*. again. "I saw you throw away your burden."

"Why have you brought it? What makes you think I wanted it?" This was the first thing that *A*. had said since the arrival of the small man.

"Why?" The small man laughed; the features in his rather expressionless face showed nothing if not an innate good nature. "I saw that you had the choice between travelling light and keeping this. I went down the side of the cutting when the horsemen had gone. I say I went, but you know how steep that cutting is. Why, I've seen men try to climb it, while they were being pursued. You can imagine what an easy target they were for the horsemen." He paused, and dropped the bundle on the floor. "It's heavy for the usual package they give you when they release you from prison." He eyed the package. "You must have had time to collect the things you had hidden before you were put inside."

The tall man, who apparently had not been listening to the conversation, turned to *A*. "How is that food getting on? I take it you're not particular?"

"No."

The smaller of the two men bent over the pack. "What have you got in it? This pack? Apart from the usual things?"

"Identity card. Provision book. The testimonial from the governor. The usual things, as you say."

"Yes, I don't doubt that. But why is it so heavy?" He looked at *A*. in a mystified manner. "Did you say that you threw it away because you didn't want it? Or just to lighten yourself?"

"I don't want it."

The small man nodded, keeping his silence. "Then do you mind . . ."

"Open it by all means. It's nothing to me."

The tall man looked down at the stirring of the stew. "At least you might need the enamel plate and the knife. They always put those in the packages. And then we might eat."

The small man was fiddling with the straps. "What's this?" He brought out a sheaf of papers in a limp cloth folder. "What's all this paper?"

The tall man took the folder from him. "He was telling me that he was a seditioner. This is presumably his sedition." He glanced at the first page. "Or a copy of it. This is all carbon copy."

"I picked it up from where it had been hidden," said *A*. "I put it on top of the things they sent me out with."

"And you want to throw it away?" The small man, who somehow gave the impression of being illiterate and therefore capable of holding any kind of writing in awe, canted his head to one side. "That makes no sense."

A. stopped stirring the stew. The tall man nodded at the pot, and *A*. began his stirring again. "No," said *A*. "It's not like that any more. It's all changed. When I wrote that there was a kind of fire in me; I couldn't wait until I had finished everything I wished to write. Now it is all different. The sense has somehow gone from it." He looked up at the two men, aware that he had been speaking predominantly to the taller of them, and even then with no degree of clearness. "I hope I can put that in a better way." He paused, and renewed his stirring of the pot. "I don't wish to talk about it. About anything else, yes. I have to rely on you." (Again he addressed the tall man.) "And I need your help." He shrugged his shoulders. "I'm lost. What else can I do?"

The tall man ignored any appeal for help. He turned to his companion. "He says he was writing his own biography." He smiled; again *A*. noticed the prominence of his eyes, with their strangely coloured irises. "It must be something if they prosecuted him for trying to have it published." He bent down and took a

couple of plates from the orange box that stood upend-
ed at his side. "It makes you wonder what he's done
in the city." He took the spoon from *A.* and liberally
filled one of the plates and, without a second's break,
plunged a fork into his plateful and began to eat,
exhaling through his open mouth, for the meagre stew
was all but boiling. "Turn out that stove. It's the little
valve at the bottom that does it."

The stove hissed and the flame went. The tunnel
was silent. The other two men began to eat. *A.* found
that his portion of the stew was small and almost
meatless and even while he was trying to pour it onto
his plate the tall man, who had eaten his share wolf-
ishly, was eyeing the pot, and even made as though
about to pull some of the remnants of the meat from
the stew. The tall man crouched next to *A.* who
sensed his hunger. The shorter man pulled half a
small loaf of bread, a dry brown loaf, from the orange
box, and offered it to the tall man, who took it without
speaking.

They kept silence while eating.

The three men ate in their own individual ways.
Each man ate, and the manner in which each ate gave a
clue to each character. The tall man, the man in the
corduroy suit, ate as though he took the meal as his
right. He had consumed the better part of the brown
half-loaf, tearing the stale bread with his long white
teeth. The small man applied the whole of his concentration to the meal, staring down at the plate. The fact
that he stared downwards was somehow significant,
and very much in contrast with his companion's gaze,

(33)

for the latter, even while eating with a rapidity which showed an extreme of hunger, glanced from time to time at the outer world beyond the mouth of the tunnel. And the third of the three men, *A.*, had retrieved the folder which contained the copy of his writing. The folder was thin. This was due to the fact that the carbon copy had been made on the thinnest of india paper, the paper upon which the scriptures are printed. As he ate he turned the pages.

The tall man looked down. "Well?"

A. looked up at him. He was uncertain as what to say. He felt himself to be very much in the hands of these two people, and yet he was unable to ask any question.

"I can see it all," said the short man. "He doesn't know what to say." He resumed his meal. "I know it. I was in there. I know it all too well. When you go in, you are taught – it's the first thing you are taught – that you must ask no question. Imagine it. It's like having a young dog, and slapping it round the head, merely because it does something you object to. It's the same there. You ask a question, even though you might mean nothing by it. The question you ask might even be a pleasantry. You might ask, as I once asked, 'Is it raining outside?'" He lifted a fork, and held it above the plate, using it to reinforce his words. "And you soon grew to know that there was no question, however simple, that wouldn't be answered by some kind of physical punishment."

"Of course," said the tall man. "We know all that. You have told us that before. That's why he sits there, eating what he's given. That's why he does the thing he does." He shrugged his shoulders. "Look." He stared down at *A*. "I know your name. I know why you are here, and I know that because of your previous experiences you can never trust us." He had seen something moving, out beyond the tunnel, but he dismissed it as he looked. The scene was familiar to him. He knew the presence of every wild animal in the cutting. "I know all this. I know it too well. And yet, when I pointed to that stove and said, 'Stir that pot' you obeyed that command as though it had originated in your own mind. I saw you take hold of the spoon the moment I pointed." He crouched down. He cast his acute gaze over the other two men. "I have the disadvantage of you here. I was never in the prison, down in the city.' He turned away, knowing that he would receive neither comment nor answer. "All I hear are the comments of those who have suffered it." He nodded in the direction of the small man. "Well?"

"Yes, that's quite true."

He looked at *A*. "And what of you? How have they altered you?"

A. looked up from his book. He had finished the small portion of stew, and he still was hungry. He might have been reticent, but the eyes of the tall man induced him to speak. "What can I say? I don't know what has happened. I don't know."

"You were young when you were taken prisoner. What has happened since then?" The tall man stood up again, and resumed his stare from the tunnel mouth. "When you were young you felt the need to write something which they thought seditious. From what you say they had been watching you for some time." He put his hands in the pockets of his suit jacket, perhaps attempting to find something to smoke. He withdrew the nub of a cigarette, looked at it, and put it back in his pocket. "Why did you feel the need to write? And what did you write? And why did you throw your parcel away with such freedom? And why are you so half-hearted about a thing that has cost you everything from reputation to liberty?"

"I don't know." *A*. leaned back on the straw which had been spread, presumably for the purposes of bedding, by the side of the dry tunnel mouth. "I have looked at the thing I had written." He pointed at the folder of india paper. "I know it is badly written. I also know that I would never write the same thing again, given the same opportunity. All the circumstances would have changed. The things which were then important are of importance no longer." He paused, looking down at the straw between his feet. He saw the small man look at the other, and he saw, through the tail of his eye, that that glance was not reciprocated. He wondered whether he should speak. He wondered whether the two men would be interested in anything he might say. He looked at the tall man, the man with the corduroy suit; in a very inconsequential manner he wondered where that corduroy suit had originated. He looked down at the folder that contained the closely typed pages. "I am lost. These things are foreign to me now. I don't know the reason why I felt such a need to write them. They mean nothing."

"You are exaggerating," said the tall man, in a tone which indicated either preoccupation or boredom.

"No, I am not exaggerating."

The tall man looked down. "You feel deeply about all this." He looked back along the cutting. "It's flattering to us, this fact that you can trust us. Unless you are speaking to yourself to ease your own mind. If that were the case, we would have to feel not only that we were poor listeners, but that we were totally supernumerary." He still held his empty plate, and he looked round as though there might be something else to eat.

"No." *A*. stood up. "I don't know who you are. I don't know anything about you. How could I? And you have asked me little. But here I am with a manuscript of mine. I barely understand it, now."

The small man leaned forward, and touched the edge of the folder with an air that suggested reverence, an action that secured *A*.'s belief that the man was illiterate. He cocked up his face, and stared at *A*. "Was it all due to the prison?" he asked. "Surely, if you wrote it, you can understand it?"

The tunnel mouth had suddenly become a silent place. The silence was broken by the tall man, who laughed, briefly, in an abstracted manner. "You overestimate the power of the prison," he said. "It's only increasing maturity that has made our friend's mind alter."

"There is truth in that," said *A*.

The tall man walked towards him. "I wonder if it

was truth? Perhaps you denigrate yourself." He grinned, and reached out for the file.

A. was reluctant to let him touch it. Here, out of the city, he wished he had never collected the package from the place where he had hidden it.

"You are a self-effacing man. You are probably correct in everything you say," said the man in the green corduroy suit. "But, if that were the case, why did such a work of writing sentence you to the city's judgement? What have you said?" He took the folder in both hands, and read the first page. He did this in the manner of a man who reads something quickly, because he knows that time is limited. He turned the page. He looked at *A.* "You have made a number of grammatical errors." He leafed through the folder. "What is there here to condemn you?"

"I was different in the city."

The tall man handed back the manuscript. "Yes, I suppose you were." Then he said, surprisingly, "I have never been to your city myself."

"That's strange."

"No, not at all. I have travelled along the railway, above the city on the viaduct. I looked down at the city: I suppose it is strange." He stood against the arch of the tunnel mouth. He was visible only as a silhouette. "Right?" He looked down at his companion.

The shorter man stood up immediately. "Yes?"

There was much in this brief action between the two men that put *A.* in mind of the action between an inferior and his master.

"There are three of us now," said the tall man.

"And I suggest we get on our way tomorrow." He suddenly turned to *A*. "It's all right. You'll do well to travel with us." He walked over to the man. "God knows, you have judged us, and we have judged you." He smiled. "We have all three of us spoken our conclusions, one way or another." He began to walk a few yards down the cutting, perhaps to gain a view of the sunset. He turned back suddenly, and pointed to *A*. "Trust yourself," he said. And then he shook his head. "Perhaps you did a wise thing when you threw that package away. You might have saved yourself some inward searching. It's always difficult to understand, in retrospect, the things we do when we are young."

The evening was well in with its encroaching darkness. The cutting, prematurely dark, was a valley of blackness while the trees on its upper banks still glowed with colour.

"There are three of us now," repeated the tall man.

"Why do you say that again?" *A*. lay on the straw, resting on his side.

The tall man looked at him. "Three for safety," he said. "An old superstition. If we press on tomorrow, then we'll need safety." He jerked a thumb in the direction of the black tunnel. "I suppose you've never been beyond it?"

"No, I have never been here before. Perhaps, when I was a child, in the train, but I remember nothing of that."

"No, that might be true. But now it's all changed. It's difficult to know what you may find. The villages beyond have a reputation for unfriendliness and inhospitality." He paused, and walked over to *A*. and sat down by his side. *A*., seeing his face in profile, silhouetted against the sky, found himself looking at that profile. The man had such characteristic features that it was possible to imagine him to have been a distinguished man; the face was idiosyncratic to the point of uniqueness. He turned to *A*. "Perhaps the various travellers who make their way along the track have made them inhospitable."

"I remember once," said the shorter man, but his colleague cut into his words, and he immediately fell silent. There was nothing reproachful in this. Again *A*. was reminded of the contrast between the two men.

"There are so many who take this track; it's so direct. It's possible, on the railway, to sit on the roof of some deserted quarry building and see a hundred or more people pass in a single day. They travel in one direction."

"Where are they going?"

"How should I know? When one has been here for some time, one never needs to bother the head about other people, unless they show some interest or friendliness first. It's easy to travel twenty miles with a chance companion and never ask his origins, or he yours." He put his hands on his knees, and looked down at his thin feet. "You learn to take people as you find them."

"But you helped me, when I was escaping from the horsemen."

The tall man smiled. "That's true. But then I had to do something. You gave so much away by your expression. It was easy to see your fear. I had to do what I could; even then, if I remember correctly, I was diffident. But normally one never questions another man. Who knows whether he would tell the truth? You meet the men with the impossible adventures. You hear all the old tales of hardship, real or false. It's like that. I suppose one grows callous with age and with prolonged travelling. Now I wouldn't give money to a beggar who told a professional beggar's tale. And there are beggars." He pointed to the smaller man. "He's a beggar. He can tell a good tale. He can recognise likely prey at a hundred yards. Isn't that so?" He touched the man in the leather coat with the toe of one of his boots.

"If you say so."

"And he's an accomplished thief." He smiled, benevolently. *A.* wondered whether he was listening to some private joke between the two men.

"If you say so," answered the smaller of the two men, his words curiously inflected. There was an easy complacency in the very way he sat.

"And talking about that," said the tall man, his voice lively. "Where's the bottle?"

"I wondered when you'd ask for that." The small man put a hand in the capacious pocket of his leather coat. The garment could have been a poacher's coat. He withdrew a spirit bottle, a dark glass thing shaped like an oversized hip-flask. He passed it over to his companion, who held it up to the light.

"The level's gone down since this morning." He uncorked the bottle. "I suppose you're going to tell me that it was thirsty, up on the top of the cutting."

(41)

"Yes, I was thirsty up there."

The tall man shrugged his shoulders, as though the comment did not interest him. Instead he looked down at the open bottle. He swallowed twice. His drinking was entirely silent. He replaced the cork in the neck, and handed the bottle back to the other man. "Tomorrow, then, we might as well set off."

A., who had watched the passing of the bottle, now followed the tall man's stare. "How do you know I'm going in the same direction?"

"Where else is there for you to go except to follow the railway?" The tall man lay back at his ease. "It's not a journey for a loner, unless he has all his wits about him. But we shall have to see. Tomorrow. When we get out of the tunnel. It's a sight that would do you good to see: the land lies flat, they say, a plain perhaps twenty miles wide, with a range of hills that are so faint that you might mistake them for cloud. And the track is as straight . . . as straight as . . ." He did not bother to finish the sentence. "It's too easy to talk. You come with us. Spend the night here, and travel through the tunnel with us. Then you can be your own agent." He paused. "You don't trust us?"

"What reason have I for trusting you? I know nothing about you. I have only seen you here." *A.* looked at the lean profile. "And as for your friend, I know nothing about him, except through you."

"That's quite true." The tall man folded his hands across his chest. "I think I said, not long ago, that these are unwelcome questions. Travellers on the road scarcely ever tell of their origins, because they know that anything they might say will be met at the best with a half-belief. It's a habit one grows into, this traveller's cynicism. It's a thing I rarely think of."

"But you have been well educated." *A.* could hear his gentle breathing. "You must be going somewhere, and travelling for a purpose."

"Oh, indeed I am. I would never dispute that for a moment."

"Then where are you travelling?"

"You'll see the range of hills when we arrive at the other side of the tunnel. If this weather keeps up."

A. was about to ask another question; he leaned forward. He opened his mouth to speak, but was grasped by one of his upper arms by the tall man. "Let me go," he said, his voice raised; he resented the touch of the man's hand.

"I want to tell you something." The tall man spoke with a sudden urgency. "You are new here. You haven't the seasoning of an old traveller; that's nothing to do with age, of course."

"What do you want to tell me?"

"You were going to ask a question."

"What of that?"

"Don't ask questions. For a start they don't help you; what help can you expect to get from half truths? And we are not here to pass the time of day." He slowly released his grip on *A.*'s arm. "We all carry our past with us. In the same way that you carry that sack of papers. In time we learn, all of us, that no other mortal is interested in what we have to say. The past of each of us is no more than a half truth. Witness the cursory way

I looked at that manuscript of yours. I don't want to read it. You will meet people on the road who profess some kind of art, and they are the most untrustworthy. The fake doctors, and the spurious lawyers, and all the rest of them. Why, once I met a man in rags who boasted that he was the financial adviser to a large bank. He was a strange one, that. His head was full of his figures. He carried a notebook with him and, in the evenings, he would amuse us by feats of mental arithmetic."

"I recall," said the short man. "We would all sit round the fire at night, and to pass the time we would shout out figures – five-figure numbers – and he would divide them and multiply them, and work out averages."

"What was he doing in rags?" *A.* looked into the darkness where the profile of the tall man was still distinct.

"What was he doing? He was like the rest of us. Trying to earn his living. It was all right for him in summer, in the picking season. He told us that he had once borrowed a good suit – he might even have stolen it – and applied for a post as a financial manager to a fruit-grower's estates. He said he was in post there for a year before they found out that he was a traveller."

"How did they find that out?"

"These questions of yours! Don't you know yet the things that are ineradicably stamped on the face of a traveller? The things that make up his mannerisms? His foreignness?"

"How can you mean that?"

The thin man sighed. "We must be up at dawn. The light will come through the tunnel." He paused, and then leaned forward and spoke to his colleague. "You will be up first, to pack?"

"Yes. I'll wake you."

Gradually they fell asleep. *A.* was unable to sleep for a long time. Once he rose, and walked a few yards out into the cutting. The night air was soft, and the eddy of air flowed now into the tunnel rather than out of it, so that it was scented with the night flowers rather than the lime and mortar miasma of the damp tunnel.

He did fall asleep, and, once he had accomplished slumber, he did not dream. The straw that had been laid down in the corner of the railway tunnel was no harder than the straw which had filled his prison palliasse. And, of course, he was free, and had nothing to fear from the city of his origins or its vigilant watchmen. He did not wake during the night.

III

They stood at the mouth of the tunnel, facing the dawn. It had taken them no more than ten minutes to pack, and another half hour to walk through the tunnel. They had not spoken yet, and all three of them knew that none of them would speak in the face of the eastern light.

The spectacle before them was truly magnificent. The tunnel emerged, blindly, halfway up a hill. The railway crossed a deep river valley by means of a viaduct of three broad spanning arches; the track then broached the plain beyond, travelling on a tall embankment.

The plain might have stretched for twenty miles or more; distances were deceptive in this light. The distant range of hills, remote and rounded, glacially formed, set the eastern skyline with a diffuse clarity. The moulded shadows, shaped and curved, flowed down the hills and into the valleys of the range, and across the plain. The floor of the plain was divided into rich fields by thick hedges in which elms grew. The noise of the farms was audible; the early morning sound of cocks and horses, cattle and other less identifiable beasts. And there were the sounds of human origin, too; the banging of a far door of a cottage, the creak of an unseen gate's hinge, the clank of cumbersome machinery.

And, beyond the farms, the villages. An observer with a careful eye might have counted the towers of a dozen churches. A telescope would have confirmed the presence of a dozen more. That telescope could have confirmed other things that might easily be deduced from a scan across the valley. The place was rich. The land was good. The people of the plain were certainly not poor – that telescope could have picked out evidence of indolence and careless husbandry. The coppices were old and choked with brush, the ponds uncleared, the hedges thick and massive and neglected. All these things pointed to a lazy prosperity.

The tall man looked down.

A., who had been observing him, saw unmistakable signs of compassion in his face, and wondered why that might be. The tall man had seemed cold-blooded enough the night before. Now he was looking down at the plain as though he felt some kind of sorrow for it.

A. wondered whether he had misread the reason that lay behind the emotion. He tried to follow the man's gaze, and saw that it rested, not on the plain itself, but on the distant range of hills. He touched the man on the forearm. "That's your home, is it?"

"Yes."

A. did not wonder at the promptness of the reply. "Haven't you been there for some time?"

"Why do you ask that?"

"You were looking sorrowful."

"Oh, that's nothing. One gets these off days." He

shifted from one foot to another. "It's all the same in the end."

The small man, who had been watching each of the others as he spoke, now nodded his head vigorously. His eyes darted about in their sockets. He pointed to his tall companion, and spoke to A. "You don't want to worry about him. He has these moods. Sometimes you'd think him a different person. Yesterday –" He shrugged his shoulders, as though the gesture would explain what he meant. Seeing that A. did not reply he went on: "Yesterday he was on one of his up moods, but coming down. I can tell these things. I could tell yesterday that we would be in for a sticky few days with him." He spoke as though his companion had not been present.

The tall man smiled a rare smile. "He's very frank. He says what he likes. He's often right. One of the advantages in being simple. An animal instinct for sure-footedness." He sighed, and his brief smile vanished. "Yes, he's right. I could tell that I was going to have something of a swing in mood; there's a certain colourlessness that precedes it." He began to walk forward. He looked down at the track, at an imaginary point ten or twelve feet beyond him. The plain and the hills beyond might well not have existed for him at that moment. All he saw was the track, and that for him might have been endless.

They watched him walk on, and stood silently themselves. A. saw in the thin man's walk a certain resignation, as though the man walked merely because the track was there, rather than out of any wish to arrive at

(48)

his journey's end. He turned to the shorter man. "He was saying something last night about the expression that forms on the face of a traveller." He paused. "Was he talking about his own expression, now?" He looked at the tall man, who, with head bowed, walked unthinkingly, following the stony bed of the track.

"Don't you know the things that are ineradicably stamped on the face of the traveller? The things that make up his mannerisms?" The small man spoke these words, but not with his own intonation; the sound of his voice was a faithful copy of his colleague's. And yet there had been nothing of intentional or imaginative mimicry about his copying of the other's words.

_A_. looked at the small man curiously. "You remember everything he says, do you?"

"Most things." The small man, shrugging again, beckoned _A_. to follow. "Yes, I have an ear for remembering certain things that people say. Particularly when they use good long words. Now, take that last thing I said to you; you remember the word 'ineradicably'."

"Yes, I do."

"Well, when I heard that one word I woke up. I had been sleepily thinking to myself. But that one word; and then I remembered the other words that surrounded it, and I saved up the phrase. It's a good one. It sounds well, when slid off the tongue. A common man like me wouldn't use it. A common man like me would sound foolish. Say a thing like that in my home village, and you'd be in a fight, as like as not. But it seems right that he should say it." The short man jerked a thumb in the direction of the slow, walking figure. "I occasionally forget words. I think I forgot a word there; what he really said was: 'These questions of yours! Don't you know yet the things that are ineradicably stamped on the face of a traveller? The things that make up his mannerisms?' "

A. began to walk. "Why do you go to the bother?" This art of remembering second-hand phrases, for the sake of their euphony and not their context or meaning, defeated him. He found it difficult to understand the small man, for it was obvious that the phrases in themselves might well have no meaning as far as he was concerned.

"It's no bother. I like to hear people speak well."

"You speak well."

The face of the small man shone with an immediate pleasure, and *A.* knew that he could have passed no greater compliment. The small man walked beside him, trying ineffectually to hide his grin of satisfaction. He shook his head. "You are being honest when you say that? Genuine?"

"Of course. Why should I not be?"

"No, indeed." The small man smiled again, and began to walk faster. Perhaps he was attempting to catch up the tall man as rapidly as possible; perhaps he wanted to tell him of the great compliment which had just been given him. As he walked he began to talk rapidly to *A.* His voice now had a sudden and slightly stilted quality to it, as though he felt himself to be under scrutiny. He looked up at *A.* "You ought to have heard me when I was alone, before I met him. I was so shy I'd hide rather than talk. Shy? I used to do all my travelling alone, at night. It was good, at the time. I would pass by the small camps that other travellers had made. I would see them all asleep by their fires, their faces sleeping with a childlike peace. I loved to see the gleam of the flames' reflections on the faces of the sleeping travellers. Even the old men were children when they slept. And the youths and the haughty young men – men younger than me – would be divested of any element of conceit. There is no vanity in any sleeping face, though there may be an emptiness."

"You are quoting him again, surely."

"Not wholly." The small man held up his index finger. "I am using the words that I learned from him, to be sure, but I'm using them to say what I want to say." He looked at *A*., as if he required permission before continuing. When *A*. nodded, he began to talk again. "Yes, I travelled alone. And I would sit at the travellers' fires at night, when they were asleep, and I would pretend to myself that I was in reality travelling with them, that I was one of their party, that I was one of them, no matter how menial a position in the hierarchy of their group I might be. But the dawn would come, all too quickly, and the first of the sleepers would stir, and the cock would crow – and I would have no option except to slip off into the undergrowth, and to continue on my journey alone. I was that shy. I knew they would ask me where I came from."

"How did you meet him?" *A.* pointed up the track to the tall man.

The small man nodded with a happy vigour. He was flushed with pleasure. *A.* was aware that he had been staring at *A.*'s face while he had been speaking, perhaps to gain an impression of the kind of reception his story would receive. *A.*'s eyes had evidently expressed the right thing.

"He was on the track, alone. His green corduroy suit was fairly new then, and fitted him less well than it does now. Well, he was on the track. I had been walking behind him, and I could only see him vaguely. I was not following him, but we were walking at the same speed. It was just before dawn. I saw that he too had been walking all night. When the dawn came he found a place to sleep, in the sun. I watched him from the top of the track and when he was asleep I went down to join him, and to sit next to him. It was as near as I got to having company.

"I told you a moment ago that I used to sit in the camps of the sleeping travellers, and that I used to watch the faces of the sleeping men. That's all that I said then, but I would have said more, except that I thought you might think it foolish and stupid of me to continue. But I say this – it's no credit to me, I know – but I was that shy and yet so very much in need of company that I would look at the sleeping men and imagine their character. It takes some doing, that. And then, in the flickering firelight, I would initiate an imaginary conversation between the sleepers and myself. I would imagine that one of them, say, an old man,

(52)

had known me all my life, and that he was a firm friend of mine. I would imagine him talking to me, and the other way round. It served a purpose. I would pull out my bottle, and have a drink and then, in imagination, I would pass the bottle over to him for him to take a drink. That is what I used to do.

"Well. I came on this man here. I thought him asleep at the dawning, and I sat next to him. I watched his face. It was as innocent as the face of any passive sleeper. And then I began to wonder where he came from. 'That's a fine corduroy suit,' I said, in imagination. I said it to myself, but in a lively and conversational way. I imagined him to look up, and smile at me, and make some imaginary remark.

"And then I looked down. I saw his face for what it was. He was no more asleep than I. He was lying on his back, in a traveller's careless position, but his eyes were open. His eyes were open, and they were staring into the sky as though they saw nothing. His face, which had seemed so restful, was full of horror and fear. I knew that I could see this only because I had been so practised at looking at other men's faces. I saw despair there; real despair. I knew that he had seen me, out of the corner of his eye, but that my presence meant nothing to him compared with the presence of whatever it was that was making him so fearful. I saw that he was shaking with fear. I knew, too, that I had been speaking aloud, frightened myself, for his fear was dreadfully communicative. I looked behind me more than once, I tell you, as though they were about to come and butcher us both."

"Who are 'they'?"

"I never knew. I somehow assumed that it was a certain group of people that he was afraid of. There was no reason behind that assumption, except that he was a fit man – I had seen that from the speed at which he walked – and fit men only die when they are killed. He certainly didn't look ill. And no natural disaster could have overwhelmed him at that moment. So his fear had to be of people, of men of one sort or another, if you like."

A. smiled a slightly mystified smile. "It couldn't have been some inner fear, could it?"

But the shorter man evidently had never thought of this in an abstract manner. "He's too sensible a man to have been half-dead through fear of hell or the like," he said. "And I didn't know what to do. So I sat by him. He was sweating, and his face was cold. I wondered if perhaps he had been taking some kind of addictive drug or other. But at that moment he passed unconscious." The small man began to mime his own actions. "So I went down to a stream, and I got some water, some cold water. I went up the bank again, and sponged his face over. I diluted some brandy, and forced it between his lips. He was breathing heavily at this time; his limbs were peculiarly stiff, and there was a slight unevenness in them, a jerking tremor, and my mind ran through all the old stories of demon-possession and the like. And then he slowly recovered his consciousness. He looked at me as though he were half drugged, or just woken up from some drinking session. He took me for granted. He pointed to the water, and I gave him the enamel cup I was holding. He drank it dry, looking around him, slightly but not very surprised to find himself where he was.

"He told me later that he suffered from a kind of epilepsy." The short man lapsed into his sincere rendition of the other's past remarks, saying, "'The neurologist diagnosed temporal lobe epilepsy'."

"I see," said *A*., who had never heard of the condition.

"It was in the stage of his recovery from that attack that I began to take to him. He was angry about nothing in particular. He was bloody-minded towards me; irrational. He began shouting at me. He demanded things of me. But that was good; it showed that he was treating me as though he understood me, and that I was at least being put to the test. I, for my part, knew that he was not well. I knew that if I put up with his irrational behaviour I would find that, when he had cooled down, he would become the normal man who I had followed.

"And, as the day grew on, he lapsed into sleepiness. I could see his upper eyelids fall over his strange irises. He slept. I remained beside him. There was nothing I could do." The short man shook his head. "I know you'll say I'm stupid," he said, "but you can put that down to my dog-like character. I am only as I was made.

"When he woke up it was mid-afternoon. I had been careful to shade his face. When he woke he saw me, and I saw his smile of recognition. He sat up and looked at me. 'I remember you,' he said, as though he had last seen me a decade ago. 'I remember you. Why are you still here?' His voice was puzzled. I could not answer; my tongue was glued inside my mouth. I could not talk. He looked at me. 'How did you manage to put up with me, a stranger? Even my family wouldn't put up with my behaviour after an attack, even though I only half know what I'm doing.'

"It was this that did it. We travelled together then. At first we did not talk. He seemed to be content just to travel with me. At length I braved a remark. I did not know how to make any kind of conversation, let alone initiate one. I did not want to talk about the weather. I did not want to betray my origins by speaking in the slang of my family. I didn't want to talk of the woman I would have married if my family had had their way. She lived almost next door to us, the oldest of five sisters; all her sisters were married. But she was too like my own family to suit me. So I chanced a brief remark. I started to speak, but immediately I opened my mouth he looked at me with his concentrated eyes, and I could no more speak than fly. He saw this. He knew he was somehow in my debt, though of course I never saw it like that. So when I tried to speak, an hour later, for the second time, he merely carried on walking. I got out the phrase at last. It was not what I meant to say at all. I remember it vividly. I know what I wanted to say, and I wouldn't have told you, because it's somehow private, but what came out was the most ridiculous phrase. 'Magnificent weather for September,' was what I said."

"What was wrong with that?" asked A., amused and disbelieving.

"Nothing. But it was the way I said it, and the meaning of it in view of all the things that had happened already. I was afraid he would turn round and laugh at me. I was standing there, ashamed of myself. I had spent so much energy in attempting to speak with this man, even this poor man, that I could only mouth some stupid comment on the weather, a phrase I had picked up, long ago, as a child. I had overheard a lady make the remark to a friend of hers. It had taken me at the time, that phrase, and I savoured the remark. I think I even used it at home, much to the amusement of my family, except my father, who said that if I spoke in that way again, in public, I would be thrashed. So perhaps I rebelled, as a child. I used to look at myself in the mirror and mouth that comment on the weather. I rebelled against my father, who was ashamed that I might be speaking another class's language in the street. Perhaps that was why the phrase was so ingrained. Perhaps that was why it came out, suddenly, when I wished to speak.

"He turned round, unsure as to his own position. Was he to nod gravely, or was he to laugh? What was his social class? Had he thought I had mocked him in some way? Had he thought that I considered him mad and irrational? He looked at me, and at that moment he could have smiled or shouted. I longed to tell him of the dumbness which had precluded my speaking with the same language my family had used. I wanted to speak to him, on his own terms. I did not want, by my non-existent voice, to bring the pointless story of my own upbringing to his feet."

"In what way was your upbringing pointless?"

"The area was pointless, and its religion, and the way in which people lived. There was decency, but it was a decency born of cant. I was expected to become a copy of my father. I was even christened with his name, which was his father's name. I could not stand the ideals expected of me. The fact that I would have to live and work and spend my life until my death in that very neighbourhood."

"And these things made you dumb?"

The short man stood for a moment; he was stationary on the track. For some reason *A.*'s question had reduced him to immobility. "Yes," he said, slowly, "I think that was the reason for it." He broke into a sudden smile. "Of course, at the hospital they said that my dumbness was psychological. That's what the duty doctor said. But of course there was no more done about it; I could no more trust them than they could me. In fact, I wasn't completely dumb; I had a kind of repertoire of stock phrases which I could use, matching each to see if it fitted a question that I might be asked. But, of course, this list of stock phrases was unwelcome at home. They were all phrases drawn from the trite conversations of the better class of people. The street conversation that we overheard, and which in truth was never meant to be conversation, but rather an idiomatic expression of public mannerism. Why these things meant so much to me when I was a child I will never understand. Perhaps they meant nothing; perhaps they were only symbols of a world my father would have denied me."

"Are you any better here?" asked *A*., abruptly.

"Yes!" The smaller man almost shouted the answer as though the question had been self-obvious. "I can at least talk. At least, when I have the courage to do so. He taught me that. You must remember that that is a very new thing for me."

They had reached the tall man now, and they walked at either side of him. He did not speak; indeed, he did not register their presence by any expression, action or gesture. Again *A*. was reminded that the tall man had said that all travellers must have the same ineradicable stamp.

The small man was leaning forward of his comrade, who walked on as though the former might never have existed.

The small man grinned at *A*. "How far we have come!"

A. looked back. The side of the hill was already distant, and the mouth of the tunnel was the size of the entrance of a wasps' nest.

They walked on. Eventually the smaller man withdrew the bottle from his poacher's pocket, and offered it to the tall man.

The tall man, still looking down at the track, stopped. The other two stopped also, and looked at him. He began to search the ground with the keen gaze of the traveller, and he shifted a large stone with the side of his foot. His hands were in his pockets. He ignored the bottle which was outstretched in front of him. The man who held the bottle smiled slightly, his smile indulgent.

The tall man spoke. "Right. We'll have a swig and a rest here. It will do us no harm; there's no hurry." He glanced at the two other men, and his face was white and colourless. "Give me that, please." He took the bottle, and drank two mouthfuls; no more. He glanced round the skyline, seeing something that made him anxious, for he pulled his coat around him. He stared at the small man, who shrugged his shoulders (his favourite gesture) and took back the bottle. He looked at *A*. "The ways of lengthening life are few and poorly known," he said. "But the ways of shortening it are universal." He looked unhappily down at the ground, as though it were the only solid thing about him. He called the small man to his side. He touched his shoulder, and bent down. *A*. heard the words perfectly, though they were not intended for his hearing.

"I'm sorry. It's not me, you understand. I think I'm going to have a fit."

*

They both looked at him.

He stared, bewildered and frightened. The short man took his arm. "I'll find you a quiet place," he whispered, "down by the side of the track." He turned to *A*. "I never saw anything like this in my ragged-arsed childhood." He began to lead the tall man away.

A. stood alone at the top of the track. It was clear that both the other men regarded the coming epileptic attack as a private and embarrassing thing. *A*., unclear as to what he might do, put down his burden and

(60)

looked along the track. The way ahead was empty; the sun had risen, and the heated ballast of the track made the air waver above it, so that the track itself became a tenuous and uncertain thing. Distances were obviously deceptive in this plain; the further hills appeared to be as far away as they had when the travellers had first stood at the entrance of the tunnel.

A. sat down. He had nothing to do. Out of boredom he opened his package and took out the copy of his manuscript. He felt the weight of it in his hand. He put it on the track beside him, and picked up the first page, not to read it but to see the print. His eye caught a line. He found it almost impossible to believe that he had written this; it seemed to have so little importance now. He lay back and smiled to himself. He wanted to dismiss the subject from his mind, but could not.

He had risked a great deal for that wad of paper. He had lost his freedom, had lost, transiently, any peace of mind. He had lost his home, for he knew that he could never go back to his home city. He had forfeited any friendships he might have made. He had been stamped with a convict's record. And in spite of all this he felt that the ideal itself had so little meaning. He tried to look back. It certainly had had a meaning, he knew that; he remembered the laborious hours he had spent, working mostly at night. It had been gratifying, then, the thought that he was producing something which would be branded as being powerful and seditious. He remembered the lamplit room in the widow's house. Why had she been so attentive and so attractive to him? Why had she looked on him as a kind of god? *A.*

remembered that he had been childishly flattered by the fact that she had read his work with the fervour of a disciple. Several times he had questioned her about the sense of the things he had written, and she had always answered him in a lucid and cogent way. He had been pleased by this. She had become his audience. It occurred to him that she would have praised anything he might have done; anything he might have undertaken. Her love was a very blinkering thing and quite uncritical.

A. thought back to that time of infatuation, aware of its insubstantial nature. He looked down at the copy of his manuscript. It had surely been written in a claustral and unreal environment. How could it mean anything, taken out of the context, not only of the city about which it was written, but of the house in which it had been written? How could it mean anything in the absence of the knowledge that its author was young and its single hearer uncritical?

He looked at the wad of pages. They certainly meant nothing here. He turned to a page that explained the inanity of a supposedly secret official procedure, a vestigial service of commitment held in the cathedral undercroft every year. This service was one of the many which bound together the church and the city state, one small item of ritual which was always listed as 'a part of the cultural and religious heritage of the city' in the official books. The dress worn at this particular ceremony was supposed to be secret, and the service itself private. The fact that *A.* had annotated the procedures which took place during this service had formed a substantial part of the accusation against him.

His prosecution had been, to begin with, mild and almost uneasily ineffectual. The fact that he had intended to publish material which purported to expose the secrets of the city's governmental workings was dwelt upon in some detail. The facts were clear enough. There could be no doubt in the court's mind as to his guilt. And then, and only then, the prosecution had brought out all the power in its command. Perhaps the aim in this was to dishonour cheaply, *A*., and every concept he had then stood for, and to stir up anger against him, so that the harsh sentence, when it fell, would not seem unfitting. The specialist evidence was brought out, the psychiatrists and the other doctors. Much was made of his affair with the young widow; of the fact that she was newly widowed; of the fact that he had lived with her. The prosecution pursued this course with an irresistible ferocity. It was only when every scrap of dignity had left the image of the seditioner that the sentence was passed. The trivial stupidity of his crime had been forgotten.

A. remembered that the official newspaper had called the sentence 'lenient'. As a show-trial, as a thing for dissuading others, the whole performance had been conducted along lines set by age-old precedents.

And now? *A*. knew that he had achieved nothing by any action that he had ever taken against the city state of his birth. The only thing he had done had been to lose any right to his home and his good character. The trial itself had taken away any sense of self-esteem. The sedition itself was meaningless. That was why he had thrown the package away yesterday.

He remembered the city with a kind of ill-directed hatred. This hatred even covered his past friends and patrons, employers and colleagues; it even covered the woman who had helped him to write.

He wondered why he should have been so mild in the presence of the two travelling strangers. He had always thought that on his release he would have been silent and unapproachable. This had proved not to be true. And the cause for this? He was unable to analyse it. Perhaps he saw something of himself in the lives of the two men with whom he now travelled. Perhaps he had a kind of sympathy with the short man's hotch-potch loquacity. And there was the fact of the epilepsy. And the fact that few questions had been either asked or answered.

*

It was towards evening when the short man returned. He stood at the top of the track. "You are still here?" he asked, his voice slightly surprised.

"Why shouldn't I be?" *A*, who had been sitting, doing nothing, turned to the man.

"I would have thought you gone. I suspected that you might have no time for us."

"No, I don't think that's true." *A*. stood up. "If I've been aloof or diffident it's been because of various things that have happened."

The short man nodded his head. He asked no

questions. It was difficult for *A*. to tell if this was out of a sense that they would not be welcomed, or whether the short man had no particular interest.

"How is your friend?"

"Sleeping."

"Is there anything I can do?"

"No, I don't think so." The short man looked at the land beyond the railway. "We haven't much food."

"Where do you find that?"

The short man laughed. "A traveller's question!" He began to look at the track, searching for a place to sit down. He saw *A*.'s papers, but did not comment on them. He sat down, watching the sunset.

The western sky was striated with orange clouds, and the light that fell on the plain was of that same deep orange colour. The colour made the green things strangely dark, while it emphasised the fields of stubble, and made the grey towers of the churches gently prominent.

*

The tall man joined them before sunset. He sat silently, looking at the western sky. His tiredness was easy to see. He made no remark and passed no comment, but sat in silence. When he moved his arms or shifted his legs it was with a weariness that would have indicated, under other circumstances, that he had just been through an exhausting physical trial.

"How are you?" *A*. leaned forward.

"Better. I shall sleep well tonight." He looked round. "I'm sorry it had to happen here. We ought to have made further progress. We've only done a few miles."

"It's all the same in the end," said the short man. "Don't trouble yourself on our behalf. I don't want you feeling guilty about it. After all, I'm only travelling for the sake of it, and our friend" – he indicated *A*. – "probably doesn't know where he wants to go, yet. So there's no hurry."

"No, that's true." The tall man was slow to speak.

The short man surveyed the land around the track.

"How are things?" asked the tall man. *A*. noticed that his suit of green corduroy fitted him well, now that he had recovered. Somewhat irrationally he wondered whether the tall man's moods were shared by his clothes.

"Very well," said the short man. "There's a farm down there, by that clump of elm; the further clump. Do you see it?"

"Yes." The tall man followed his gaze. "If you're going down there, we might walk on and let you catch us up. We'll have a fire going."

"Good." The short man stood, and, with a brief nod first to his companion and then to *A*., began to climb down the steep bank of the railway. His descent of the bank was nearly silent.

Immediately he had gone, the tall man turned to *A*. "You are very quiet."

"Where has your friend gone?"

"Down to that farm."

"To beg?"

"No. Of course not. They'd never listen to him; they

(66)

never listen to any of us. I thought I had explained to you how ingrained is the inhospitality of the people round here, both in the villages and in the towns."

"Yes, I remember you saying that."

"He's gone down to find us something. We might as well move on." He began to stand up, somewhat unsteadily. "We'll have a fire ready for him when he returns."

They gathered their belongings and walked up the track for about a mile and a half. They stopped under a clump of new ash. Here, under the tall man's direction, *A.* gathered the material for a fire. He brought armfuls of wood from rotting trees he had found at the base of the bank. When he returned he found that the tall man had searched the track for the wooden keys which had long ago held the vanished rails in position on the removed sleepers. *A.* crept down the side of the embankment again. He found a wooden boundary post that he was able to uproot.

The tall man stood over the pile of wood, evidently satisfied at the amount they had collected. He began to make a fire.

Distantly they heard the sound of a shotgun. *A.* jumped to his feet. He made no sound, but faced the tall man who now rested by the fire, half asleep. "What was that?"

"He has obviously found a hen-run."

"Shall I go down and see what has happened?"

The tall man looked up; he had been staring into the fire. "No, it'll be all right. We've had a few newcomers join us on the track. Usually they just smile when they hear a gun firing. Sometimes they wink at me. You are different. You have shown a concern for him." There was a sardonic inflection to his voice.

"And why not? He was telling me about himself this morning. His dumbness. His meeting with you. He was telling me about his travelling along the track, and his night-time vigils at the travellers' camps."

"Oh, I don't doubt that. He's a good talker." He raised himself up on his elbow. He stared at *A*. "I thought at first that you were bright," he said. "It's difficult for me to know where your brightness lies. Sometimes you seem only half intelligent. You're credulous. Too believing."

"Well, why not?" *A*. sat by the fire, opposite the tall man. "He told me the truth about other things. I know that for certain. He would never have the motive for telling lies."

"Oh, they're not lies he tells. They're half lies. Or half truths, if you like. Whether he thinks they're truth or knows them to be lies doesn't matter. I'm sure you find the same thing yourself. Don't you find yourself stretching a story? Passing off some other man's anecdotes as your own? Of course you do. And so do I. And I daresay, were you to read that tract of yours, you would find, in the light of further experience, a great deal of it to be half truth or half lie. You must have written it according to the falsity of the circumstances in which you found yourself. After all, we all live under false circumstances. And just as circumstances must colour our judgements, so they must colour our interpretation of fact."

(68)

There was a great deal of this that applied to *A.*, and he wondered how much he had given away of himself while he had been speaking to the other man.

But the tall man was speaking again. "It's easy to see. Give me no credit. You wrote your so-called seditious material when you were a young man. It's easy to see that. You were a dissatisfied young man. It's easy to see the things that coloured your thoughts. You are a very subjective writer."

"You were reading it last night?"

"Early this morning. I couldn't sleep."

"Oh." *A.*, seeing that his manuscript had been read, remembered that he had made his intention of throwing the thing away obvious. It was impossible for him, therefore, to complain of the fact that the tall man had read it. "What did you think of it?"

"A difficult question. So much depends on the context. I don't know your city. I've never been there in my life. It sounds a harsh place, but then I've only your word for that. And you write subjectively. The sense of what you have written must also depend on what you were, and how you lived, at the time. That is, if you wish your work to stand as fact rather than fiction.

"Indeed, I'm a poor judge. I sometimes think that there can be no such thing as factual work. Perhaps the passage of thought through the head and any attempt at communication makes any idea fictional."

A shotgun sounded for the second time; the sound was followed by diffuse echoes.

A. jumped to his feet. "What is happening down

(69)

there?" He stared into the darkness, but saw only the horizon of the featureless plain.

"Have trust. He's a cautious man. If he dies on this track, it won't be because of some foreign farmer. He's a very careful man. When he approaches a chicken run he knows how long it will take before the hens start to make a noise, or before the yard dog barks. And you yourself know how silently he can move. He would put down his silence to the fact of his previous shyness, when he used to travel by night. I would put it down to the fact that he's a born thief, a thief for the sake of thievery. He's good in the chicken runs, he is. I've watched him throw stones to disturb the foliage. The farmer then lets both barrels fly. Then he fleetly escapes.

"My guess is that that second shot was one of exasperation, aimed at nothing. He'll be getting a few potatoes together now."

They fell silent.

The night closed round them, and the fire glowed hot. *A.* built a little bank of stones to the windward side of the fire. He glanced at his companion. "This reminds me of my childhood," he said.

The tall man shrugged his shoulders, a gesture that reminded *A.* of the smaller man. He wondered how many of each other's idiosyncrasies each had acquired from the other.

"Yes, I suppose it would," said the tall man. Then he drew in a long breath. "Were you there this afternoon?"

"When?"

"During the fit?"

"No." *A.* looked at him curiously. "Why do you ask?"

"It's embarrassing. It starts off so mildly. A minor mood swing. I think I know when I'm going to have a fit about a day before it happens."

"I see."

"Temporal lobe epilepsy, they called it. It starts off with a depressive mood change." He pushed a piece of fence wire into the fire, purposelessly, and watched it glow to red heat. "Before the attack I get an aura. A strange word; means nothing."

"Your friend described it to me."

"Oh, no doubt he exaggerated." The tall man leaned forward. "He tends to exaggerate things. Perhaps it's due to the rate he lives life. He's a very active man. Enthusiastic to take things up, and then keen to forget them. How he has stuck to me I don't know."

"What is your aura like?"

The thin man shot him a keen glance. Then he relaxed; perhaps he had expected a barbed question. "I don't know. It's not a thing that's at all easy to describe. Or perhaps it is. At all events, were I to describe it to you, you would end up with a very different thing from the experience."

"That makes sense."

A figure could be seen, further down the track. The small man had returned. His darker silhouette against the dark sky was unmistakable. *A.* stood up to welcome him.

"What have you found?" asked the tall man, sitting and looking upward.

His companion was too short of breath to reply. He lowered the two chickens and the rabbit to the ground. He patted his poacher's pockets, and brought out some potatoes. He squatted down. "It becomes increasingly difficult," he said. "But tonight we'll have the rabbit. I'll skin him and gut him now."

"I have some wire to skewer the joints."

"Good."

There was something professional about their manner. Hardly an action or a word was wasted. *A.* sat back and watched them. It was clear to see that they had been in each other's company for some time – it was even possible that they were related – and *A.* was struck by the efficiency with which they carried out their tasks. It seemed impossible to imagine that they were travelling without a purpose.

He would have liked to ask the question 'where are you going?' but he guessed that the question would be unwelcome. And, he reflected, the question would have been unwelcome to him, also.

IV

They continued their journey by night. As if to aid their travel the moon was full, and the track ahead of them was radiant in the pale silver light. The distant hills were obscured by a falling mist. That same mist, hugging the ground, obscured the fields of the plain, and only the topmost limbs of the trees and the railway embankment were visible. The mist lay over the plain whitely, like a blanket. There was no wind. They made good progress. They talked little.

They walked for four hours, covering fifteen or more miles. Neither of A.'s companions showed any sign of tiredness, though A. himself, unaccustomed to this unusual exercise, felt the weariness of his feet. Besides, the track itself was difficult for him to walk on, for he was not used to it. Whereas his companions took the irregularities of the path in their stride, used to walking this track, A. found that he frequently stumbled over the potholes left by the vanished sleepers on the permanent way.

As though they knew A. to be unfamiliar with the track, both the other men were considerate towards him. Once the short man looked at him. "You must be done in," he said.

"No, not at all." It was evident, from the strained way he said this, that A. was not being truthful.

They continued to walk.

At something nearing three in the morning they came upon a small band of travellers asleep by a fire, the embers of which glowed dully. *A*. would not have seen the sleeping men until he had stumbled on them, but the short man evidently possessed some instinctive sense which the newcomer to the travellers' life did not have. He sensed the presence of the camp some time before they reached it. The short man touched *A*.'s sleeve, as though warning him to walk with care.

The three of them stood looking down at the sleeping band of travellers. The strangers, all asleep, lay in what seemed to be uncomfortable attitudes, their faces turned to the dying fire. There were five of them: an old man who could not have been a day younger than seventy; an equally old woman; a younger man, about *A*.'s age, lay in the arms of a woman. Perhaps they were husband and wife. The woman's hand lay across the shoulders of the young man, and a ring glimmered in the light of the dying fire. Beside them lay a child, wrapped in blankets.

The three newcomers looked down at the sleepers, saying nothing. They had approached with utmost silence.

A. looked at the two men, and saw the gleam of the firelight on them.

The shorter man began to whisper. His voice was so soft that, were it not for the intense silence that lay over the track, his words would have been lost. "You can see how it was," he whispered, looking at *A*. "I was telling you about such people as these."

"Yes."

"Keep your voice down," whispered the shorter man. "You don't know who they are. I've never seen them before. Though you can see that they are used to travelling. Look at the old man."

A. looked at the old man. He lay asleep, though it seemed that he was only on the verge of sleep. The slightest sound would have wakened him. His face, seen now in repose, had a dignified look. He slept with his mouth closed. His full beard was pale and silver in the moonlight. His eyes were only lightly shut.

It is uncertain why the old man woke; certainly it could not have been any noise that the standing travellers might have made. Perhaps the old man woke coincidentally. He opened his eyes. His face assumed a wondering expression, though he had not seen the three standing men. He yawned, and his yawning was protracted. He looked across, beyond the fire, looking at the faces of his sleeping family. His gaze rested on each of the other sleepers. He looked at the face of the young sleeping woman. Although it was difficult to tell in the firelight, it seemed that it was she and not the young man who was his blood relation. Then he looked at the young man. He smiled slightly. His gaze rested on the child. Then he put out a withered hand, as if he wished to wake up his own wife, the old woman who slept next to him. Perhaps he wished to show her the peace that lay in the repose of the other sleepers. But he did not wake his wife; his hand dropped by his side, and he closed his eyes again.

The three standing men looked at one another.

Then, as though acting together, they melted into the undergrowth: the ragged bushes that lay along the surface of the track claimed them without a sigh.

They walked away, the tall man with his long strides, *A.* close behind him. The shorter man walked with some reluctance, as though he had found it difficult to leave the sleepers. When they were about a quarter of a mile from the camp of the sleeping travellers, he paused.

"What is it?" asked *A.*

The short man resumed his walking. When he spoke it was with some reluctance. "Do you see what I mean, now? About the beauty of the sleepers? Do you have an inkling of how I felt, when I was dumb, when I could only sit and look at people like that, and feel no compulsion to speak?"

"I think I do," said *A.*

*

They rested for a few hours. They had travelled another five miles. The tall man stopped, suddenly. "I have been told about this place," he said. "There's a village not far from here. We'd better rest here, and press on tomorrow. I don't want to sleep near that village."

"Why?" *A.*, questioning as ever, spoke abruptly, the word close on the tail of the tall man's remark.

"Why? I'd have thought the answer would have been obvious. Haven't I told you of the hostility of these villages and towns?"

"Yes," said the shorter man. "I made that mistake once. It was not pleasant. Have you seen the village dogs? And the village children? How they treat vagrants and travellers?"

"No, I have not. But surely," continued *A.*, "if you do no harm, how can they feel such hostility?"

The shorter man sat down, next to his tall companion. "One can get a bad name," he said. "I was telling you. I once slept by mistake near a village. I was woken most fearfully. Have you ever seen the villagers stone a traveller? I was lucky, there. If another band of travellers hadn't turned up and felt some fellow feeling for me, it would have gone ill with me. It made it worse, of course, the fact of my dumbness."

"We might as well sleep here," said the tall man. He lay down, on his back, his hands behind his head. He stared at the moon.

"What do you do when the bad weather sets in? And the rain?"

The tall man lay at full length, one ankle crossed over another. "What do you think? There are barns not far from the track. And there are the huts that used to belong to the railway. Some of them have stoves in them still; grid-iron fireplaces. Some of the windows still have the glass in them. And, if you look for it, there is still coal to be found along the track, if you care to look hard enough. Still, it's no easy life. Of course, you can sleep under a railway arch. There are worse places than those. Some of the arches have niches in them where you can comfortably sleep. It's easy to get hold of hay."

(77)

A., following the tall man's example, lay down to sleep. He was weary, and the discomfort of the track here was mitigated by the profuse growth of a plant that, appropriately enough, turned out the next morning to be bedstraw. He lay on his side, using his package for a pillow. He looked along the track. There was no sign of life. The stars were bright.

They slept until the morning sun awoke them. The sun was high; they must have slept on well past the dawn.

*

They made a lazy start to the day. The mists of the previous night had dispersed, and the morning had already grown hot.

A. woke to find the tall man scanning the horizon. The short man was nowhere to be seen.

"Where is he?"

"Down there. There's a river. He'll be washing himself."

"I think I should do the same."

"You'll have to hurry. We must be on our way."

A. went down to the river to wash. As he stood by the bank he saw the small man drying himself on a piece of clean sacking, a needless thing, for the sun was hot enough to dry him in a few minutes.

It seemed expedient for *A.* to ignore him; he stripped and dived into the river.

The water was cold, and the exercise invigorating.

He swam to the opposite bank, turned and swam back again.

"You have some soap?" the small man called.

"Yes. They gave me some in my pack."

"Hang on to it, then. It's precious stuff, here."

A. stood on the shingle, soaping his face and body before returning to the water. He stood in the water, up to his chest in it. He gripped the muddy bottom of the river with his toes; the current was stronger than he had supposed. He looked at the small man. "How far away is this village?"

"Two miles. It's a large enough village. A small town. I don't know its name."

*

They came to the village at about ten o'clock. As they approached they saw the square tower of the church, and later the roofs of the buildings. The village was beautiful. The golden stone of the houses blended with the red roofs.

They walked rapidly.

"What is there to be afraid of?" asked *A*.

"Who said anything about fear?" The tall man looked ahead of him, staring down the line. He gave a cursory glance at the village. "We're best out of it. They're unfriendly, from what I hear. There's a strong feeling against travellers here. Besides, the Provincial Magistrate has made his home in the place."

The short man pointed to a large house, about half a mile away. This house faced the railway. It was a tall structure, four stories high, but rather narrow; it gave the impression of a transplanted town house. A parapet hid the roof. "That's where he lives. He's notorious."

"Why should that be? What harm have you done in this village?"

The short man looked at him; apparently the question was unwelcome. "Nothing," he said at length. "Nothing of importance."

It was becoming clear to A. that the travellers possessed a number of odd superstitions about the railway on which they were walking, and the land through which they were passing. He had asked many questions concerning the supposed hostility of the villagers and townsfolk of the places through which the track passed. All his questions had been met with vague and indefinite answers. No concrete reason had been given. He remembered the various superstitions that he had been told during his journey. It was possible that the supposed animosity of the villagers was yet another superstition. He kept his silence as they approached the village.

The derelict railway transected the village. The embankment ran on, straight as a die, making no allowance for the presence of the village. The main road of the village ran under an impressive arch cut in the embankment. A., standing on the bridge, looked down at the village. The other two men, seeing him stop, grasped him by his arms.

"Come on!" cried the short man, but in such a subdued tone, and so muffled with anxiety that A. had difficulty in understanding him. The tall man tugged at his sleeve.

"This is surely no place to stop," said the tall man. Although his voice, unlike that of his companion, betrayed no anxiety, it was clear that he too was agitated.

A. saw no reason for either anxiety or agitation. He looked down at the village, and saw the empty street. Nothing was moving. The church clock tolled the quarter. Nothing else happened. No people were visible.

"Why do you call it a village?" asked *A.*, for indeed the place was more like a market town. He saw the town square, flanked by tall houses. A red-brick building, incongruously placed at the narrow end of the square, protruded a portentous portico into the street. The words 'Town Hall' were inscribed on the arch that surmounted that elaborate portico.

"It's no more than a village," said the tall man. "Come on. We must go. We have been lucky so far. Far luckier than we deserve. We haven't been seen yet." He was speaking rapidly. "It's quite true that the villagers will never come on the railway; they have a superstition that to venture onto the track will make them travellers like ourselves."

"How do you know all these facts that you call superstitions? How can you know these things? Have you ever been into the town here?"

"Of course not," said the tall man. "You must trust me. That's all I ask of you. I once asked you to refrain from questioning me about the life of a traveller; that matters nothing, now. All I ask is that we make a move immediately, and get out of the vicinity of this place. As I was saying, they won't come onto the railway, not even the police, but they can still throw stones. There's nothing to stop them using shotguns, too. We are most vulnerable here. Just come with us. I'll answer any question you may care to ask there." He began to walk away.

"The place is certainly quiet," observed the short man. "What day of the week is it?"

"Tuesday," said *A*.

"You remember the day, do you?" There was nothing ironic in the way the short man spoke. While he did so he leaned against the wooden parapet of the bridge. He was evidently waiting for *A*. to make a move. And then he crossed his hands. He smiled indulgently, as though about to put forward a reason that would be clear even to *A*. the newcomer, a reason why they should quit the town as rapidly as possible. He leaned further back to settle himself.

"Do you know the name of the town?" asked *A*.

The small man flung his arms out. For a moment *A*. thought that he had done this out of exasperation, but he saw even in the second that he looked that this was not so. The man was suddenly frightened, very frightened. He struggled forward.

They saw the reason for it. There was nothing they could do.

The rotten wooden parapet had soundlessly given way. The rail was now sagging backwards, over the void beyond the bridge. The small man had attempted to save himself by flinging his arms forward. There was nothing he could do to save himself. The rotten woodwork had given way under his weight. His face, blanched, stared down at the solid ground. He made a move to grasp the rotten rail.

And then, with a cracking sound, the woodwork gave way, and the man fell forty feet to the road below.

They stared down at him. He lay on his back, one leg crumpled under him. The treacherous wood of the decayed parapet lay around him. His head lay to one side, the neck twisted and deformed. Blood had started to trickle from his scalp.

A. began to run down the track to the steep grass slope. He began to clamber down, half falling, half running. He heard the voice of the tall man behind him. "Wait, you fool! Come back! What good can you do now? Can't you see his neck's broken?"

A. looked briefly up at the staring figure of the tall man. He said nothing. He reached the level ground at the bottom of the bridge. He ran under the shadow of the arch. He saw the rotten wood from the parapet lying about the distorted body. He knelt down. The man was still breathing, but with a peculiar waxing and waning respiration. The eyes were open, and the pupils were dilated. The eyes stared straight ahead, looking at nothing.

The street was still empty. *A.* looked up and down, towards the town hall, beyond the bridge to where a few cottages stood. He looked down at the man. Where to find a doctor? The doors of the houses were resolutely closed. He stood up, prepared to run to the nearest house for assistance, but, even as he prepared to run, he looked down at the body.

The eyes stared sightlessly. Respiration had stopped.

V

A. sat on a ragged horsehair couch that stood in the vestibule of the town hall. He had been told to sit there.

Less than half an hour ago he had been standing on the railway above the arch of the bridge and staring down at the open doors to the darkness of the room where he now sat. Now he looked back to the railway bridge with the broken parapet. In the shadow of the arch stood a group of unmoving men staring down at the body of the dead traveller, now visible in the confined shadow. As he looked he saw that they made way for a horse and cart which came from a street beyond the railway arch. He saw their distant gesticulations. The body was loaded onto the cart. The men dispersed; the street was silent as it had been when *A.* had first seen it. The fact that the woodwork of the bridge's parapet had a gap in it was irrelevant.

He looked back into the vestibule. It was a high room, featureless except for an upward running staircase, a lift lattice and a number of brown-painted doors. The place had very much the look of an impoverished institution – the walls were painted a cream gloss down to the level of the door handles and below that a narrow black line descended to a dado of chocolate brown. The paint was peeling and near the floor the plaster bulged with damp. The interior might have been the interior of any of the six workhouses within the city.

Without warning the lift descended. The gates clattered open and two men emerged. The Mayor's official, the man who had told *A*. that as he was the only witness to the death he must remain seated on the horse hair couch, held the gates open for the other to get out. This latter was a fat man of intermediate height. *A*. wondered if he was the Mayor; there was the slow manner of provincial dignity about him. The other man fussed about him, rubbing his hands together, bowing from time to time. He was doing the speaking; the Mayor was ponderously silent, aware perhaps not so much of his own importance as of his own presence.

A. stood, half out of deference.

"You're still here. Ah." The official looked briefly towards *A*. "Perhaps, if you would wait a moment –" His voice was staccato and noisy. He turned to the Mayor. "I'm sorry, sir. The car had instructions to be here for eleven."

"It's gone that," said the Mayor. Although his voice was slow and even sleepy he spoke the words as though each had an individual significance. There was a grunting quality to his speech that did not appear to arise from the vocal chords.

The Mayor stood at the door doing nothing but watching the empty street. He played with the gold albert which spanned his waistcoat. His black coat was long and his trousers were unpressed and wide. He was aware that *A*. was watching him, for he turned to the official. "Is he waiting to see me?" He waited for a reply, his face expressionless.

"No, no," interjected the thin man, who, unable to keep still, was shifting his meagre weight from one foot to another. "I told him to sit there. He witnessed the accident."

"The man who fell from the bridge." The Mayor dismissed all thought of *A.* and resumed his stare through the door.

The car drew up. The Mayor walked down the steps and got into the car clumsily, revealing a square yard of shiny black trouser bottom as he did so. He lay in the leather seat. The official closed the door and the car drew off.

*

The sequences which had filled the morning were apparently unlinked. *A.* had been an audience to each one. He felt that he might as well have been an audience at some blackly repetitive but disjointed morality play where the moral was beyond finding. The small traveller had died; he had died in the midst of his loquacity. Had he done something to deserve death? Had his death been precipitated by the breaking of an unknown code?

A. waited another hour on the horsehair couch and then, suddenly, he stood up and faced the open doors. He walked out into the sunlight. He stood in the square and looked up at the houses and the shuttered shops. There was nothing abnormal about the town.

He walked down towards the archway of the bridge, looking up at the track as he did so. He saw the untenanted line of the track as it lay along the grassy ridge of the steep embankment. He saw the line of tilting telegraph poles running out into a perspective higher than the highest chimneys of the houses. He was about to walk to the side of the stonework, already raising his hands to pull himself up the embankment when the sight of a figure standing on the road just within the arch made him halt.

It was undoubtedly the Mayor.

The man came out from the shadows. He squinted up at the sun and the fingers of his right hand touched the rim of his felt hat. The sunlight picked out each speck of dust on his faded black suit. The face was the Mayor's face but how subtly it had changed.

"You're the priest as well?"

The other man smiled tolerantly. "It's not uncommon," he said, "for the mayor to be the pastor in the provinces." He pursed his lips, thinking perhaps of some task he had neglected to do. He shrugged his shoulders. "In fact I'd say it was almost universally true." He began to walk towards *A.* who resisted the temptation to retreat from him. He took the traveller's arm. "Where are you from?" He seemed not to recognise the prison discharge suit.

"The city. The terminus."

"You've travelled a long way."

"Not at all. Two days."

The Pastor's face cleared. "Of course, you took the railway. That's different." He paused. "I've just been

(88)

to conduct a service for the man who fell from the bridge," he said, conversationally. "If I'd known that you were his fellow traveller I could have told you while we were in the town hall together. It seems a pity, a profound pity, to say the service over the body of a stranger. You could have shed some light on his origins." He began to walk up the road. "Did you know him well?"

"No. We met by chance."

"You don't know where he came from?"

"No."

"Did he tell you anything about his family?"

"Yes. He told me his story; I was never sure how much to believe. I think he was romancing a lot of the time. Not that it matters now."

"Why did you leave the city?" As a mayor the man had seemed to possess the foibles of a provincial mayor. As a pastor he had a cleric's. It was difficult to imagine any fundamental alteration in the man.

"I was driven out, Father."

The Pastor continued his walking. "Don't call me 'Father'."

"But you are the priest of this town?"

"No. I am pastor, mayor and magistrate. That is all. There is nothing sacerdotal about my appointments."

*

The Pastor held *A*. by the arm. The old man's grip was soft and compliant and *A*. could find no reason for shaking off the man's hand: he was unsure whether the

(89)

Pastor held his arm because he wished to guide A. towards the portico of the town hall or whether the Pastor wished to support A., thinking perhaps that the young man might be exhausted. It was possible that the Pastor himself had some kind of bodily infirmity and that he touched A.'s arm for his own support.

As though the unwelcome shadow of the dark vestibule had affected A. in some way the young man shivered as he asked: "Why are you bringing me here again?"

The Pastor smiled with an easy complacency. "I can tell there's something wrong. It's your manner. You're shivering." His words were studied.

A. expected the Pastor to point to the prison suit but he did not do this. "I've found from experience that you can't rely on what travellers say. I would like more justification than your word. You have come from the city?"

"I've told you so. What other proof can I give?"

The Pastor conceded the point by nodding his head slightly. "What are your plans now? Where are you going?"

The question was unexpected. The Pastor's voice had been low and distinct: A. felt himself to be under close scrutiny. He had to make the decision as to what he would tell this man. He wanted to equivocate. He could have shrugged his shoulders. Instead he put his hands together in an attitude of prayer but there was nothing supplicatory about his posture. "I'm going on."

"I see." The Pastor spoke with a renewal of that

blend of complacency; the distinctness had gone from his voice. "Where? Have you any destination in mind?"

Again this question was unexpected, although it should not have been. Again *A*. was offered the choice of a refusal in his answer, or an abject denial of any knowledge as to where he might be travelling. As it was he looked out, and took a step forward, and pointed to a further range of hills, which, truth to tell, seemed no closer now than they had done when he had first stood at the entrance to the tunnel, many miles back. "I had intended to go there. I have a friend who lives there." He was aware of the falsity in this; he had merely been echoing the tall traveller's words.

The Pastor had not bothered to follow the direction of his gaze. "Oh well. Then there's a certainty in what you say. I'm pleased that you know where you are going, and where the railway leads."

A., still looking up at the hills, heard the sound of the lift doors being opened in the hall of the building. He turned round to see the Pastor standing in the lift. He took a pace towards the man.

The Pastor, seeing him walking towards the open lift doors, made no effort to close them. "Yes? What is it?" Although he had asked a question, his voice had an element of final dismissal in it.

"Wait, will you."

"What is it? There's no need for us to talk further." The Pastor began to close the outer door. "If you know where you are going, then you'll do well." He paused in his closing of the door. "I hope everything goes well

(91)

for you." He put his hand again to the door of the lift. "It was only because I thought that you seemed to have some inner uncertainty that I brought you up here." He smiled, and *A.* was unable to fathom whether his manner was feigned or genuine. "However, we can all be mistaken. Good luck to you."

A. stood hesitantly in the hall. He stared at the Pastor, who had closed the doors of the lift, and who was now about to press some unseen button on a panel of the lift wall.

"Wait," said *A.*, his voice urgent.

The Pastor, perhaps recognising the urgency of the voice, pulled his hand down, and opened the lift doors. "Come in," he said, beckoning with his hand. "Come in."

A. got into the lift. The Pastor closed the doors, and the lift began to rise.

The walls of the building slid past the gratings of the lift. *A.* gripped the black metal lattice-work.

"Why did you ask me to wait? And when I waited why did you pause?"

A. made no answer.

"Oh, I can see you're a traveller," said the Pastor. "Make no mistake about that. You don't deceive me by pointing into the distance; that's only a kind of involuntary temporising."

A., perhaps angered by his complacency, turned to face him. "What business is that of yours? Why should you take an interest in me? Do you know who I am?"

"Which question would you like me to answer? And don't raise your voice. I've already given you the benefit of the doubt by saying that you temporised. Others might have called you a liar."

A. looked at him, indignant rather than ashamed.

"I beckoned you into the lift because you hesitated. That was important. The fact that you shouted 'Wait!' was of less importance." The Pastor spoke rapidly. "As to who you are . . . how should I know?" He smiled, secretively. "I see a constant stream of travellers. It's pitiful." He tilted his head on one side. "Have you ever seen them? The poor ones? It's all very well to talk about goals and ambitions, but this finger-pointing! Speculation: they don't know where they're going, whether they're pushed from behind or drawn from the front, but they're always pat with their answers. Intelligent or stupid they point to that empty horizon."

"It's not empty. It's beautiful, at least in certain lights."

"Don't give me that stuff about the moonlight over the mountains and the dawn sky." His voice had been raised; now he spoke quietly. "No, you're putting on an act. You haven't begun to deceive yourself yet."

A., who had been listening carefully to the Pastor's words, put a hand to the lever of the lift. "Nothing you say will change me. I have nothing to say to you; I must get out of this town of yours."

"Don't touch the lever." The Pastor folded his arms. "The lift is programmed to accept the first order."

A. looked at the man with irritation. "I'll have to go with you then."

"How much money have you?"

"What business is that of yours?"

"Everything. Are you a vagrant?"

"No! Let me get away!"

The lift stopped. Someone outside pulled the doors open. The Pastor pushed *A.* out into the hallway.

A. stood sullenly, his arms crossed and his legs apart, looking at the hall as though the place was no concern of his while he was beyond any stretch of its jurisdiction. It was only when he saw the three clerks that he moderated his idea of independence and sufficiency. He looked at them, each of them in turn, aware of their steady stare. He took a step backwards.

*

For all the unfamiliarity of his surroundings, *A.* found that he could not take his attention from the Pastor. He had seen the Pastor as a typical image of a priest; he had seen him as a provincial mayor. And now he saw the cerebral nature of the man. He saw the Pastor speaking to his subordinates and, for the first time, he knew that he was in the presence of a magistrate.

"What do you carry?" asked the Magistrate.

"This package?" *A.* attempted to resume something of his air of uncaring independence.

"That package," said the Magistrate.

"I must go," said *A.* faintly, for he was feeling the stare of the clerks intolerable.

"The stairs are there," said the Magistrate. His voice had the edge of tiredness. "You'll be escorted back to the street. Meanwhile, let's get the formality

(94)

over with." He walked towards a wooden-panelled door the width of which was disproportionate to its height. He had no need to beckon *A*., for the young man was at his heels, anxious to escape the three clerks and to interpose the solidity of the heavy door between their stare and himself.

When *A*. followed the Magistrate into the room beyond the high door, he expected to be interrogated as he had been interrogated at the time of his trial in the city. He expected perhaps an emotional play upon half ascertained facts, a directed series of questions, skilfully put, that would leave him no alternative but to give an expected answer. He expected also that he would be scrutinised in a biased light and, perhaps of greater importance, that he would accuse himself of his answers to preordained and fixed questions. Most of his accusers at his trial in the city had been priests; this man was also evidently a priest, though he had called himself 'pastor' and had denied any priestly function.

The reality of events in this room was not the fixed and unalterable reality of his city trial. This was not obvious from the beginning. The fact that the Pastor or, as *A*. now thought of him, the Magistrate, had pulled out a comfortable chair and gestured for the traveller to sit in it and had offered a glass of wine to the young man cut no ice. *A*. had been used to comfortable antecedent approaches before a condemnatory attack.

A. sat warily. He refused the wine. As far as he could he maintained silence. He answered in indefinite monosyllables when an answer was necessary.

The Magistrate was patient; *A.* observed the man, and knew that his patience was not feigned.

It was this unfeigned patience that won *A.* over to the man. *A.* felt his heart warming to him. In a moment of silence he leaned forward, placing his hands on the Magistrate's desk, looking down at the fraying cuffs of his own jacket. The Magistrate, seeing that the young traveller was about to speak, leaned back in his chair.

"I've done you a disservice," said *A.* He said this, and then he shrugged his shoulders. "I'm sorry for that."

"You've been diffident and curt, that's a fact," said the Magistrate. He rested his hands on the arms of his chair. "And you've been evasive, too. You've been interrogated before."

"Many times." *A.* looked at him. "How did you know that?"

"I saw the questions you expected to be asked the moment you closed the door on the clerks; the transient relief giving way to something else as you saw this room with its bare table and its two chairs." He looked up. "You are on the railway because of the accusations."

"Yes."

"And being a vagrant is preferable to returning to your home city?"

"I don't think I could return."

The Magistrate stood up. "Would you like to remain in this town instead of returning to the railway as a vagrant?"

"What do you mean?" *A.* looked at him. "Stay here?"

"It's possible. Work's easier to find here than in the city."

A. remembered the clerks. "I couldn't stay here."

"You think the past would catch up with you here?"

"I don't know." He smiled to himself. "You'll say I'm temporising now I've said that." He looked at the desk top. It was completely empty. The leather of its surface was faultless and unscored; nothing heavy had ever rested on it. Then he saw the light coating of dust. He ran his finger along the surface of the desk surreptitiously, under the cover of his other forearm. The Magistrate was speaking again.

"Yes," said the Magistrate in such a manner that *A.* wondered whether he himself had drowsed and missed the beginning of a sentence. "We get a good many vagrants in the town. Not so much in summer perhaps."

A. looked up. He stopped his tracing on the dusty desk. "I thought they avoided the towns and villages."

"Not when they need us." The Magistrate smiled his slow smile. "Your reticence tells me that you've heard too many conflicting tales already."

A. resumed his tracing in the dust. "But the other travellers were not false with me. It's hard to put it, but in a way they were more false with themselves."

The Magistrate paused in thought over *A.*'s last statement.

This feature of his, this fact of his listening ability, this consideration of the sparse remarks which the young traveller made must have been responsible for his gaining *A.*'s confidence. When the Magistrate

(97)

spoke it was with deliberation. He appeared to have a wise maturity. He tried neither to sway A.'s mind nor to disillusion him.

"Shall I enumerate some of their superstitions?" He looked interrogatively at A. "There's little point in doing so, but it may clarify things and help you be on your guard in the future. They have a superstition that the further they venture from the railway the greater is their danger. They accept this, yet at every opportunity they are ready to thieve from farms and to beg in the towns in winter. Again, they have a superstition that the townspeople do not or cannot walk on the track. That's a false superstition. Who do they think buries the vagrants that die? Last winter I was summoned to the burials of more than a dozen. Most of them had died through exposure because of the superstition that they couldn't get off the railway without risk to themselves."

"You contradict yourself."

"Why?" There was a mild uplift to the voice.

"You said that the travellers were only too willing to come down to the town when they were starving. Now you say they would die on the track rather than come down."

The Magistrate passed a hand over his brow. He looked suddenly tired. "One can't generalise," he said. "People differ. Hunger and superstition drive different people different ways."

"Yes," said A., slowly. "I see that." He looked up. The Magistrate was smiling to himself. His smile was not the smile of a man in an advantageous position. It

(98)

was the smile, the apologetic smile of a tolerant man who has found that a chance visitor has discovered dust and who is polite enough to refrain from commenting upon it.

For the first time *A*. was free of his suspicions. For the first time he was aware that he was being tested as an equal and as a man without stereotype.

With the stiff gait of an old man the Magistrate walked to the side table and returned with the dusty decanter and two glasses

*

The Magistrate had nothing further to say; for the last half hour they had been content to sit with the wine, unhurrying, scarcely speaking. The Magistrate skirted the major questions; perhaps he knew that to ask them would be profitless.

He stood, indicating the door. "Go your way." His voice with its impractical tolerance reminded *A*. of his father's voice. Even the implied vagueness of the sentiment was similar.

A. backed out of the door and into the hall. While the Magistrate's valediction was still in his ears he searched the hall with his eyes, seeking the clerks. The hall was empty. He summoned the lift, but, as he heard the motor begin to wind, he had no wish to be trapped in the cage and he ran down the stairs, two at a time, until he reached the kitchens. As he ran he was ashamed of himself for his own duplicity. He had seen the Magistrate's tolerance and had seen in it a weakness. The Magistrate was growing old and was acquiring the limited aspiration to easy and narrow horizons. There was a certain naivety about this. There had been the simplicity of an old man's fondness: the wish that another should do well and should expand, adventitiously, those horizons. Immediately he had seen this weakness *A*. had taken advantage of it.

The Magistrate's wine was still wet on his lips when he slid round the half-open kitchen door. The smell was enough to alter his mode of thinking. He forgot the man who had wished him well.

VI

He had eaten his fill at the kitchens and his pack was weighed down with food; here was subsistence for a few days. He stood on the railway, on the bridge above the town. The track lay before him. The cloudless day was on his side, or so it seemed. A quarter of an hour's walk took him beyond the parish of the town, and the plain reasserted itself. Alone and with his feeling of independence he walked on, along the railway. Along his path he saw the ashes of many dead fires; some not long extinguished, some ancient. Once he saw a group of people lying by the side of the track in afternoon sleep. He avoided them, circuitously walking round a grove of newly sprung elder. He walked on for another mile and then he knew he was alone.

The sense of loneliness approached him only when he had exhausted the first eager anticipation of continuing his journey. He looked ahead at the range of hills which, in the afternoon light, had taken on an aspect of obscure distance. He stopped in his walking. A moment before he had been striding eagerly in the manner of a man seeking a destination; now, on seeing the flat plain ahead and seeing the distant hills, he stopped. Almost involuntarily he sat down, heavily, tired by his exertions. He sat on a low wooden box which must have once formed part of the signalling apparatus of the defunct railway. Strands of wire and the cut ends of metal rods still extended from this rotting artifact. He looked about him and saw nothing but the rich agricultural lands of the plain and the railway, and the hills beyond. He opened his pack and took out the food he had managed to procure from the kitchens. He remembered the tired face of the cook, a small woman of middle age, a woman who had been glad to pack food into every pocket of his pack and coat. He remembered her face; her friendly eyes had been searching. Then he had only thought of food; now he saw her face. She had brought out great dishes of cold meats and had sliced off lumps of meat, wrapping them in greased paper. She had asked no questions. With each of the things she had shoved into his pack she had muttered some trivial endearment.

A. wondered how he must have looked to the woman. Tall, hesitant, diffident? Foreign?

The cook had been working in the kitchen when he had opened the door. She had been wiping down the great preparation tables, opening cupboards, pulling drawers. He remembered every word that she had said, but he saw in his mind's eye her searching face, framed with dyed hair. He recalled the touch of her hands as she had stuffed his pockets with food.

Now he pulled a piece of boiled bacon from his pocket and began to eat it. He was not hungry. His action was instinctive. He had been thirsty rather than hungry and the taste of the salty bacon exacerbated his thirst. Immediately he felt his thirst he shoved the piece of bacon back in his pocket and looked for water.

A half mile more and he found a stream which ran under the railway. He climbed down the embankment and stood at the side of the stream. The brook wandered through tall banks of sedge and marsh and then vanished into a culvert which, characteristically, had been built disproportionately large for its purpose.

He stood on a baulk of blue brick. Having assuaged his thirst, he looked down at the mouth of the culvert and saw that the stonework was still perfect. The fronded ferns at the other side of the track reflected their greenness in the flowing trickle of water.

After he had drunk he paused on the baulk of brickwork at the entrance of the culvert. He adjusted his pack – heavy now with food – and then he climbed back up to the summit of the embankment. He stood facing the hills. He was aware of a change in the prospect of the day; for a moment he was at a loss as to what had caused it. Then he saw that the line of hills had altered.

He remembered that range of hills as being clear and distinct. Now they were wavering and opalescent in the heat of the afternoon; but for the memory of them they might have been mistaken for a bank of low cloud. The sun was on the decline and the shadows were lengthening.

It was hardly the time for continuing a journey but *A*. walked forward, his eyes staring down at the ground in front of him, as if he wished for no further indication of his path. The stones of the derelict railway and the preordained track of the embankment were enough; he did not raise his eyes.

Thus, staring at the ground and not beyond, he overtook a fellow traveller. So closely had he been examining the ground of the track that he was unaware that he was in another's presence until they were almost abreast.

A. looked at the traveller and recognised the tall man. It was evident that *A*. had not been seen by him; the tall man stared ahead, his gaze resting on that shifting area of the track, about twelve feet in front of him. *A*. clasped him by his arm.

The tall man turned suddenly, his expression that of a man abruptly startled; he did not recognise *A*. immediately.

"You remember me?" *A*. ran in front of him, trying to intercept his gaze. "What are you looking at?"

The tall man smiled. "So there you are. I wondered when I would see you again." His arms hung loosely by his side. "I've been through it, I have."

"Have you? In what way?" *A*. began to open his pack. "Are you hungry?"

"It was his death," said the tall man. "His death has taken away a good deal of the meaning from my journey." He eyed *A*.'s pack. "What have you got there? Where did you get that?"

A. allowed the tall man to see the things he had been given in the kitchens. The tall man's hands pried into each one of the pockets of the pack. His presence was very close. *A.* took a step away from him and brushed away his inquisitive hands.

"What's the matter? Don't you trust me?"

A. smiled and shrugged his shoulders. "Where are we going?"

The tall man, suddenly interrupted in his examination of *A.*'s gain, pointed abstractedly along the railway. "We have a few hours of light left. We might make twelve miles."

They walked on, side by side, saying little to each other.

Once *A.* paused.

"What is the matter?" The tall man halted, and turned back.

"I was thinking of your companion."

"Oh. Yes. I hadn't known him for very long."

"He seemed to think a lot of you."

"He was always prone to exaggerate things."

A. shook his head. "But what does his death mean to you? You must have been together a long time; he had adopted so many of your mannerisms."

"Yes, that is true. I had noticed that." The tall man spoke, but it was evident that he was eager to press on. "We can make a few more miles yet."

"I'd be happier if I knew where we were going," said *A.*

"What had they been telling you in that town? They are very persuasive. All these small parishes ever think of are their own parochial affairs. Nothing more than that. I suppose they told you that the object of your journey was illusory."

"Yes," said *A*. candidly. "They did tell me that."

"That would be just in character," said the tall man. "They have no conception of things beyond the boundaries of their own parishes."

"Why do you say that?"

"I know it to be true."

"Then where are you going?"

"Look," said the tall man. "I can only tell you one thing: I am going up to those hills. Perhaps you can't see them well now, but you have seen them. It's the memory of them that counts and all the things you have heard. This is what matters. I am going there." He looked at the terrain about him. "We might as well stay here for the night, if you are travelling with me. Otherwise we might go our own separate ways."

"No, I would like to travel with you. After all, the track is narrow and I'm more or less forced to."

"Good." The tall man's voice was sincere. "I'm pleased about that. Then we'll stay here the night. We'll travel on tomorrow. Get up at daybreak. It won't be far." He looked up and down the track. "Is it worth making a fire, do you think?"

"Yes, I think so. It's cold."

"Yes, they say it grows colder as you approach the hills." The tall man smiled slightly as though he recognised the superstition that lay behind the statement. He set down his own pack and began to look for material with which to make a fire.

*

It was dark.

The two men had eaten, and they sat, looking at each other, the glowing remains of the fire between them. The night was silent and nothing moved; a pale moon stood on the horizon but it was too feeble and too enshrouded by cloud to illumine anything.

The tall man stretched his arms, flexing and stretching his fingers. He arched his back and put his hands behind his head, in the manner of a man who had just eaten well. "You'll do well here," he said. "I'd never have guessed it. What did you tell them, to make them give you that food and of their own free will too? And you said that you saw the Magistrate himself!" He shook his head. "He's a notorious man, or so they say."

"He was a very shrewd man. And pleasant," said $A.$, aware that, by sharing his food with the tall man, he had put him under something of an obligation. "I found no need to lie to him; at least, I knew that he would be able to detect any lie I might have told; any exaggeration that is, because his manner was such that I could not lie to him. He would have detected it. He is a shrewd man."

The tall man stirred the fire with a stick. "Well, perhaps he wished to win you over to his side," he said.

"I don't understand what you mean. You talk about the people who live in the plain and the people who travel along the railway. You imply that they are two different kinds of people. That can't be so. The Magistrate said as much. He told me some of the superstitions of the travellers, and I was forced to admit they were false and unreasonable."

(107)

"Well, of course he would tell you that. What else could he do? He had no option and you said he was a clever and convincing man."

"Have you ever met him?"

"No. How could I have met him?"

"I thought it possible. He said he had been on the railway himself to see to the welfare of the travellers. He was telling me about the state of things in the wintertime, when the travellers went down to the town itself to beg. He told me that." The tall man made a grimace that indicated nothing. "And, by the way, I suspect he also used – I think I'm sure of this – the word 'vagrant' where I would use the word 'traveller'."

The tall man leaned forward. There was a certain tolerance about his attitude, a tolerance that reminded *A.* slightly of the Magistrate himself. *A.* knew that any explanation that the tall man might make would be reasonable and forthright, at least on the surface. He prepared himself to listen.

"The fact that you say that," said the tall man, "shows that you have been listening to the kind of talk which confronts the travellers who stay away from the railway. Very well. I can only put my own point of view. That is, if you will listen to me."

"I'm very willing to listen to you."

"The fact that he summed us up as 'vagrants' shows that he does not understand the need for our journeying. That's a fact, as I see it. You might be in a position to see it, when you have travelled as long as I have done. You become used to these terms of abuse. You become used to being labelled as a vagrant. Who cares about a word? Perhaps we are vagrants. It makes no difference to us. We still continue our journey. I hope to continue on my own journey, here, along this track. And who's to stop me in that? Some provincial magistrate calling me a vagrant? I know that you've seen me at my worst; I fully admit it. But don't you see that it was my illness which forced me to start my journey? The fact of it? The fact that I could no longer stay at home? I was unpredictable; a disgrace; a blot. One can't have fits conveniently, to suit others. And, afterwards, there's a period when I'm not sure what I do. The neurologist called that 'post-ictal automatism' but that made it no easier. I think my family thought I was disgracing them deliberately. The last time my family gave me a public function was on the day of the funeral of a rich uncle; I told them that I was going to have a fit but they made it clear that there was no option but for me to get dressed in that dark suit. One of the servants helped me dress –"

"You had servants?"

"Yes," said the tall man irritably. "Of course we did, not that it matters in the least now. But I couldn't go on and I couldn't absent myself. My test had come. I would fail in my duty whatever path I took. I could imagine my nephews circling their fingers round their temples."

"Is your family close?" interrupted A.

"Not very. They're too suspicious of each other to be close, though they direct business to each other. But I was dressing. There was a voice outside. My sister, the married one. She spoke in a hushed voice.

'Is it a migraine?' she asked, foolish girl. She was too concerned with her own deportment to think properly."

"Why are you telling me this?" asked *A.*, for the story seemed to have been told many times before.

"The sake of it, I suppose. Listen to me first and see if my reasons for travelling have nothing to do with yours. Draw your conclusions when I have finished. The fact of the matter is –" he shrugged his shoulders, apparently unwilling to continue.

"Carry on," said *A.*, leaning across the fire.

The tall man stood, slowly, and looked down at *A.* "I was only telling you how I came to be up here, travelling along the railway."

"Have some more to eat." said *A.* "Sit down." He looked at the other man with anxiety and saw that tears had formed in his eyes. "Carry on with your story."

"I only know what they told me afterwards; I remember nothing myself, except that someone supported me as we walked through the cemetery to the railings which marked the family's vault. The story was told me later; some thought it humorous; others were too embarrassed to speak to me." He stopped speaking.

"Go on."

"There's not much point. The story varied with each person who told it me. I have never pieced it together; there were too many versions.

"It's easy to think of illness as either something curable or something that inexorably worsens. But when it strikes at random it's different. The week after

I was able to conduct my own affairs and sign my name and lift a knife and fork without an atom of tremor – do you think they would believe I was normal again? No. That one occasion had shown them up." He took up a lump of cold beef and began to eat. He had regained much of his composure. Again *A.* was aware that this story was a story told to others; the choice of phrase, the studied repetition all pointed to the fact.

"Think about that," said the tall man. "Think about it. It might not be dissimilar from your own tale."

"That might or might not be true," said *A*.

"Yes, it bears thinking about; the fact that you were yourself imprisoned for something that now has no meaning to you. Now you too are precluded, as I am, from returning to your home. You too are a traveller. You have no option but to continue along this road.

"You see, there is something remarkable about the life of the traveller. I suppose that you heard from the Magistrate of that little town nothing but denigration of what he would call 'vagrants'."

"Not in the least. He was considerate and understanding. He was concerned as to the welfare of the travellers."

"Well, so it seemed to you. That's probably only the impression he wished to make to you and, to judge from what you say, he had set about it in a very shrewd manner. No. The thing that's remarkable about the life of the traveller is the fact that each traveller is unknown to the others. He can introduce himself as being who he is; he can introduce himself as the fiction he thinks he is. No other traveller knows the truth about him. He could have committed what crimes his home accused him of, and yet he can talk to his fellow traveller with a spotless reputation. His past is his own; travelling companions are the friends of a moment. They do not care overmuch about him, but then one has no real friends. Let me question you on this. How many friends supported you when you were found guilty and afterwards, when you were convicted?"

"I had two friends."

"I see. And those two friends visited you in prison?"

"Yes, but I refused to see them. Eventually they no longer made any attempt to visit me."

The tall man smiled. "That's to be expected. That's all in order and as it should be. And why was it? Why should they see a man in prison? Because they felt forced to? Of course."

"Have you ever seen a healthy man with a healthy family, where his family have friends? Call them socialites, if you wish. They visit their friends often and they receive many visitors. Now imagine the man of the family struck by some chronic illness, some illness which is undignified. Imagine him on his sickbed, surrounded by medical aids to allow him to crawl to his bath and his bed; a house with his illness at its centrepoint. See, in that case, how the visits stop. How the friends fall away. How the chronic and undignified nature of the illness of that man precludes friendship."

"I've never known anything like that," said *A*.

"Well, you can take it to be true. And it remains true even if an illness is periodic, such as is mine. But the crux of what I have to say is this." He spoke slowly now, giving *A*. time to digest what he had to say.

The black night was suddenly cold and their stock of firewood was low. The tall man drew his coat about him. For a moment *A*. wondered whether his companion was about to mutter the old platitude that the temperature was sure to drop in the proximity of the further range of hills. But the tall man did not say this. He chose his words carefully and *A*., drowsing now and warmed by the food he had eaten, had difficulty in keeping his eyes open.

"You must continue as a traveller," said the tall man, "otherwise you will drift into some town or other and remain there; no doubt you will be received with open arms at first, because of your aptitudes. But sooner or later the fact of your past experience will gain on you and catch you up; you will find that you will have been judged in your absence and you will find that that judgement will not be in your favour."

A. looked up. The moon had, as it were, shaken itself free of the cloud and had risen in the sky. The hills beyond showed, with a silver beauty, their rounded summits and their shaped valleys. The range of hills stretched across the horizon and their distant splendour seemed to be both ephemeral and timeless.

Both the travellers looked at the hills as they lay down to sleep.

The night grew colder but winter was far off and there was, as yet, no touch of frost in the air.

VII

The range of hills was perceptibly closer. The air was colder. The embankment of the railway had risen to meet the lowest of the valleys with a slow and steady gradient. The track still ran on, straight and without deviation, as if it were the permanent part of the landscape and the valley had been later created for the railway to travel through.

In the shadow of a roofless stone hut, such as might once have been used by the permanent waymen of the Eastern Provincial Railway, an old man sat by a fire. It was clear that he had been travelling alone, for he had an air of self-contained independence about him. His pack was close to his side. He had this travelling worked out; his steady grey eyes beneath their bushes of grey brows were always on the lookout. The direction in which his eyes gazed had no correlation with anything he was saying, as if he looked with half his brain and saw with half his brain and, with the whole of the cerebrum he mixed the input of his failing five senses with the sureness of experience. It was obvious that he had been travelling for many years. *A.* sat across the fire from him, looking at him. His observations of the old man were very much the observations which have just been told, but it is very probable that he observed much more; he must have seen things that, when written, would have been laborious in their reading and unimportant in their communication. Following this statement, therefore, it is necessary to say that *A.* was in a much better position to ascertain the truth or otherwise of what the old man was saying. The old man was clearly no fool, for all the fact of his years' travel. Perhaps, though, that was not strictly true; some degree of foolishness, of senile futility might have been apparent in the fact that he had been eager to speak and that he had been less than eager to listen to anything that *A.* might have had to say or to comment on.

"I have been making my way along this track for well over ten years," said the old man. His voice was lively and virile and at variance with his apparent age. "I made my way out before the railway first closed ten years ago I think, though it may have been longer."

"Ten years," said *A.*

"Ten years," repeated the old man, making something profound out of the simple statement. "Since that time I've spoken to many and listened to many and all I can say is that no place is a place to stay. Stay in one place and you might as well be travelling backwards." He jerked his head back in the direction of the city. "Once I stayed for a year or more in a stone hut, out there. It was a stone hut, like this thing here, but it had a roof to it." He indicated the structure behind him. "But that was no good. I soon found that as I stayed, and the longer I stayed, the more I drifted, in thought at least, to my old home."

"Why did you start travelling?"

For the first time the old man put on a look of vagueness; he feigned deafness, cupping a hand to his large ear, though it was clear from his expression that he had heard *A*.'s question. "Yes," he said at length, judging the lapse of time since he had last spoken, "I did a foolish thing in staying in that one place for so long. You get a feeling of security which can never be real. Why, it's like accumulating things; gathering them up; making an estate; getting things together. You know that you might be considered prosperous and many of them are, down in the plain, but equally well you know that there'll come a time when your will is read out, with you dead and your prosperity in vain. Though there's more to it than that. Of course there is; there's many a justification for a man to take this track. Probably there are as many reasons as there are men travelling. I have only to think back to the times when the railway ran. Do you remember that?"

"I was told that I had once travelled on the train as a child, yes, but I remember nothing of that. It was only what I was told."

The old man leaned forward to tend his small fire; never before had *A*. seen so small a fire glow so hotly and yet be so conservative of the scant fuel that was to be found in the environs of the railway. The old man was about to speak again; there was a premonitory trembling of the lips, some inward rehearsal of the coming words. "I remember the days of the old railway," said the old man. "I remember them. The signal boxes, with their great glass windows and their white

(116)

painted finials; the signalmen themselves, seen vaguely through the glass of those windows. Why, I remember at the end of the great viaduct, over the city, there was such a signal box. I remember it well. Perhaps the base of it, the stonework, still stands?" He looked questioningly at *A*.

"I didn't notice it," said the young traveller.

"No, perhaps not. Time may have altered things. But I remember that box, because it was high up; high above the viaduct and the viaduct was high above the city. I got to know the signalman there well. He was, well, he would have been, when I was your age, I suppose, a middle-aged man. I remember him talking about his retirement. He used to talk about his retirement and his garden, down in the city, and the church he used to go to and the allotment he was on the list for. I could never understand all this. After all, he was the highest of all things; he looked down at the embankment and the viaduct and the city. He was above all things. The city was spread out below him, like a map, or as though seen from an aeroplane. But that did not concern him. Perhaps his years there, in that box, had taken away any feeling of awe that inevitably overcame a stranger such as myself. He would sit and look at me, half amused, as I peered from the window of his signal box. The height of it was frightening to me. The steps ran in a long zigzag up the white-painted posts to his box." The old man shook his head. "But there was never a man more conscientious. Have you ever seen the inside of a signal box?"

"No."

"Well, I don't know. I don't know much about these things. The telegraph system. The coded ringing of the bells. There were two bells and two dials, I think, all mounted on a dark wooden panel. And the signal levers." The old man allowed his head to sway from side to side, a curious senile mannerism that gave his voice a sing-song quality, as though he were intoning rather than speaking his words. "Theirs was a solitary life, the old signalmen. They sometimes used to go odd with solitude. The very neatness with which their boxes were kept; nothing to be touched with the fingers, only through a cloth; all the brasswork polished and all the woodwork likewise. And the gleam of the windows! I remember the man I was speaking of, one day when he was cleaning his windows with some white liquid. He didn't mind the height. He was concerned with the neatness, the cleanness within the box. And who can blame him? It was his home. He was no traveller. He was due for retirement and he was looking forward to the time when he could retire to his city cottage in some terrace. He told me his address, but that I can't remember. His name also escapes me, now. But it was the feeling of his proprietorial pride, his air of satisfaction at the neatness of the signal box of which he was master. His logging of the trains. He would only allow certain travellers up there . . ."

"There were travellers even while the railway was still running?"

The old man seemed surprised at the question. "Of course," he said. "Didn't you know that? The travellers used to walk along the platelayers' track. It was illegal then, of course. You had to get down when you came to a signal box that was manned by an officious bastard. Not all signalmen were like that, of course; some of them liked your company, and they kept an eye open for you: you could go up to their signal box with some small present, perhaps a few eggs that you'd found, or something like that, and they'd allow you to have a brew up on their stoves and get yourself warm by their fire in winter. Some of them used to allow you to sleep in the lower storey of the signal boxes, the room where the mechanism was. It was a better place to sleep than under a bridge or in a culvert." He smiled slightly, the reminiscence being pleasant to him. "It was good, that. You'd hear the man pacing the floorboards above your head. You'd hear the grate of the signal levers; in the moonlight you'd see the rods move, in your half sleep. You'd hear the single tang of the signal bell. The tapped reply. The distant clack of the semaphore arms. The coming thunder of the train.

"Of course, in my youth the railway was even more important. There were few travellers then. The railway seemed so permanent then. Way beyond your city . . ."

A. leaned forward. "I thought the railway stopped at my city. That the city station was a terminus."

The old man laughed. "No, never. That was never so. In your lifetime maybe, but I come from far beyond . . ."

The old man began speaking again, talking about the isolation of the signalmen; of the fact that even the permanent way employees regarded the signalmen as being solitary and idiosyncratic. Now the old man was talking of rumours of accidents; now he was talking of individual men he had once known, describing them in detail, and apologising for his forgetfulness as to their names. But *A.*'s thought was directed elsewhere. He had for the last day or two entertained the perturbing notion that perhaps his own city had not been a terminus or a starting-off point. Now he knew the fact to be true.

He did not know why the fact should fill him with a sudden fear, but fear was there. He looked across at the old man, wondering how much of his sudden fear he had transmitted; the old man was still speaking, though his eyes were slyly fixed on the young traveller's face.

Why a sudden fear?

A. had known since the beginning of his travelling that the end of the railway would be an unknown thing. All his questions on that point had provided no adequate answer. Now, and only now, he knew that he had started out from no definite starting point. The railway ran as far backwards as it did forwards.

A. suddenly looked at the old man. He looked at the aged face; the mouth was still muttering. "Tell me," said *A.*, interrupting, "where the terminus is."

The old man had been speaking; he recognised the interruption, and his voice stopped. The sounds of the growing evening impinged on the two sitting men. The graveness of a tranquil evening had fallen, and the two men, one old and one young, were revealed as being no more than an old man and a young man. There was nothing more. The old man, interrupted in his speaking, stood up. Now, standing, he was revealed as being of a far greater age than an observer might previously have reckoned. He bent down and picked up his few belongings.

"Where does the railway originate?" *A*. asked the question, but expected no answer.

"Keep the fire, if you like. There's a bit of wood behind the hut." His voice was not unkind. Perhaps he had heard *A*.'s question so often that he no longer saw any point in making an attempt to answer it. He looked down at the young man. His attitude might have been the attitude of a tolerant sage to a youth who has yet much to learn, but it was difficult to tell; the light was failing.

And then, with a slowness during which the darkness deepened, he made his way down the track, towards the distant hills.

VIII

The tall man in the green corduroy suit returned to the place where he had left the young traveller. *A.* was not there. After a cursory glance down either side of the increasingly high embankment the tall man resumed his stride. Apparently he was able to forget *A.* as easily as he had been able to forget the earlier companion of his travelling days. He walked easily, his strides long. His pack was light. And, as before, he looked not at his eventual goal but at the shifting portion of the track a dozen yards in front of him. He was, in that twilight, nothing more than a walking figure. His destination might or might not have been known; that knowledge was only in his own head. To an observer only the kinetic reality of his long strides would have been apparent.

He came to a disused hut by the side of the track. The configuration of the hut was difficult to make out in the fast falling light. A moon had risen again, and it gleamed through the unslated rafters. The sight made him pause. It was the black bulk of the stonework of the hut that precluded him from seeing *A.* immediately.

A., leaning against the wall, had seen the tall striding figure far off but, for some reason of his own had been content to keep his silence, and to allow the tall man to continue. Truth to tell, *A.* himself did not know what to do. The choices were clear; he could call to the tall man, and resume his forward progress, or he could wait until his fellow traveller had passed, and then make a further decision. He looked down at his feet. The old man's frugal fire was long since extinct, and its very ashes were cold.

The tall man halted, and looked about him. *A.* could see his angular profile very clearly. He knew that he himself was unobserved.

A. saw the tall man pause; he saw him looking about, as though he considered this a satisfactory place to spend the night. He heard his slow breathing. He saw the man sit down and, unmistakably, he heard him sigh. He saw the two hands raised with fingers outstretched; perhaps the man was going through some strange ritual of his own. But the two hands, pale in the moonlight, merely clasped themselves together, and then clasped themselves round an unseen knee. The half-seen man lowered his brow.

There was something so hopeless in the tall man's present pose that *A.* knew that he could not continue in his company for any longer than was necessary. It occurred to *A.* that perhaps the tall man gained his energy from his companions; that alone he was depressive and anxious; that, in company, he was able by his own loquacity to suppress this depression and anxiety. *A.*, feeling that he was semipurposefully intruding his gaze by staring at the darkening figure, looked along the track. The moonlight was beginning to dim. High frost clouds obscured the moon's face.

Almost involuntarily *A.* walked forward. He saw that

the very first step he took, the first sound of the flints of the ballast of the track, caused the sitting man to turn round.

The tall man must have recognised his silhouette, for *A.* was outlined against the sky. At all events any emotion that might have been construed as melancholy or depression left him; he rose to his feet immediately, his arms outstretched. He tilted his head to one side. "So there you are! Where have you been?"

"Nowhere but here."

The tall man looked at the hut, that roofless shell that stood vacantly in the moonlight. "I thought you might have walked on."

"Why should I have done that? There's no reason for that."

"There's no reasoning with you!" retorted the tall man, but in a friendly rather than an accusatory manner. "I wish I knew where your stubbornness lies – but that's another thing." He gestured to the ground. "Tell me what you have been doing."

"You want to travel on with me?" asked *A.*, half humorously, half dolefully, sitting down beside the tall man.

"Why not?" He opened his mouth to yawn; his teeth were very white in the fading moonlight. "What have you been doing? Not talking to one of the trackside philosophers?"

"Who are they?"

The tall man laughed. "Oh, it's an expression. But they can be most beguiling. They all have their own ideas, their own rationales, their own devices for making the evident obscure. They are like the cant-men. Once I met such a trackside philosopher; he kept me from my journey for two days, talking to him. Not that he said anything useful. He was telling me the usual things. He was drawing the analogy between the length of the railway and the passing of time. That's an old story. But he had a new front to it. He was talking about the existence of concordant generations on the same road, each travelling at the same pace. I forget the gist of what he said. I only remember that it was disturbing to me at the time; but that was two years ago. I'm older than that, now. I believe what I like, and think what I like. It's better than any idle speculation." He looked more closely at *A*. "What is the matter? You are shivering. What have you been doing?"

"No, I am well enough."

The tall man laughed again. "I should say you are. I should say that indeed. After all, who am I to talk to such a seasoned traveller as yourself? After all, you have the food. It was you that got the food from the very house of a magistrate. And enough food to feed a family, too."

"No, I met an old man. He left here some hours ago."

"Oh, yes? An old man alone?"

"Yes. He was very old; I was walking on, and I saw him here, this afternoon. He had a little fire. He was crouching under the shadow of this hut; he seemed to subsist on nothing; he had very little with him. I offered some of my food, but he only took a little; he said that he had his own methods of doing things."

"I know him. We have crossed paths often enough.

Did he talk all the while? Question you, but give no answers?"

"That's true. He did."

"He talked overmuch about the railway, in the old days, when it was still running?"

"He did."

"That's the man, then. He means no harm. He's well known; he continues at such a slow rate along the track that, unless he gets a move on, he'll never get there. He's frail enough as it is. Last winter he was sheltered, I remember, by a good-hearted band of travellers; a family. A curious family, I think. They helped him last winter. Without them he'd have been in some parish cemetery or other, with a cast-iron cross over his grave. Have you seen a travellers' corner in a parish graveyard?" He expected no answer to this, for he went on: "He'll never get there, unless he speeds his pace."

They sat talking in the moonlight, talking of nothing remarkable. Neither of them was particularly tired.

"It was strange, you meeting that old man."

"Why so? It was hardly possible for me to avoid him. His fire was by this hut."

"Ah, yes, but tell me this: where was he when you first saw his fire? Was he beside it?"

"No, come to think of it, he was not. I stood by his fire, warming myself. I wondered who could have built that fire. It was only when I had been standing there for a few moments that he came out from behind the side of the hut; there is a little thicket of bramble and elder there."

The tall man lay down, using his pack for a pillow. "Well, that's a thing in character. He's a shy man, for all his age. You'd never think him shy, because he talks so much. It says a good deal for you that you were able to gain his confidence."

"Why? He only saw me by his fire."

The tall man turned to face *A*. "Well, perhaps he's shrewd and experienced enough to sum you up from that."

"How can he tell? I haven't shaved since I left the city. I must be in tatters."

"Well, so you are. But he must have liked the look of you. As I said, he's a shy man." He sat up again, as though he had suddenly remembered something. He took up his pack, and opened one of the pockets. He pulled out a bottle. He passed it over to *A*. "Plum spirit," he said. "It's good stuff."

"Where did you get it?" *A*. opened the bottle, and drank. The spirit was neat and warming.

"Why should you care where it came from? That doesn't affect its quality, now. Besides, I owe you something. You've shared your food with me."

"That hardly matters."

The tall man took back the bottle and drank from it himself. He did not wipe the neck of the bottle; perhaps that would have been against what he regarded as a spirit of friendship. "It matters a great deal, as you'll find out, later." He paused, and began to speak again. The taste of the spirit had made the sound of his voice more restful. He was at his ease. "Why that old man should be so reticent, I don't know. There are rumours, of course. There are rumours that he has money sewn inside his coat. Of course, one never knows whether these things are true. It's certain that he has something to hide."

"Never mind that," said *A*. "It all comes back to the same question. You said, just now, that at the speed he was travelling this old man would never get there." He lay on his side, staring at the moon. "What did you mean by that? When you said that he would never get there? What did you mean by that word 'there'?"

"Oh, it's a figure of speech," said the tall man. "It's in common enough parlance on the track here. One often says of a laggardly traveller that he will never get 'there'. It's only an expression."

"I suppose that that is rooted in some kind of superstition? The place is riddled with superstitions."

"Yes, that is true. Of course, you have only been travelling for a relatively short time so you wouldn't be expected to learn the full number of the various superstitions. Neither would you be expected to know the full number of expressions that are used by the travellers. The expressions they use when they are in the proximity of the village people and the townsfolk. I suppose you could call it a kind of slang. Complicated to understand. The origin of these phrases is very old, and intermixed with it is the railway jargon of the old Eastern Provincial. That is, of course, because many of the early travellers were in the employ of the Company. Now they are mostly gone. It's very seldom that one sees a man who was once employed by the Company. But there's a kind of slang speech in common use, perhaps less so now. It was all to do with proof of identity, in the early days, when the railway was still running. This speech of which I speak was, I suppose, originally intended to identify the *bona fide* traveller.

"Of course, that matters little now. You take each traveller as he comes. Caution is necessary on both sides. Usually a traveller speaks straight. In fact, the old slang had more or less died out and, when one meets a man who speaks it fluently, one is rather inclined to be suspicious of him, because he must be – he has to be – affecting a bygone tongue.

"To come back to the point. You said to me that I had made a certain remark. You reiterated my statement that the old man would never get there unless he increased his speed of travel. You asked me the reason for saying that. It's quite natural that you should, for how can you be expected to know, without being told, the meaning of that phrase? And when I tell you that I was only speaking a form of words that I had heard, that I had absorbed, without knowing its true meaning, then you'll have to believe me. Of course I don't know his destination. He alone knows that. And, as you have seen, and as you have heard me say, he is very reticent with the information he possesses. That is to say, the information that is important. Right; concede that point. You heard him talking about his past experiences. That's very true. He is prone to do that. He will talk at length, as I am sure you heard, about the time when he travelled during the operation of the railway. You will have heard him speak of the railway, with its semaphore arms and its signal boxes. He will have told

(129)

you, as in the past he has told me, about the reticence of the signalmen, people, I might say, who had vanished long before I became a traveller. He will have dwelt with a good deal of emphasis, if indeed the old man you met is the one I'm thinking of, upon the permanency of the signalmen, with their polished brass and their polished wood, and their white-painted boxes, and their gleaming windows. He will have dwelt nostalgically on the fact of this polished brass-work, those quivering dials, those long rods that led to points and to semaphore arms which seemed then so permanent. Was that not true?"

"Yes, he told me about that."

"Quite. I knew it. We are speaking of the same man. But he said not a word of his own origins, nor of his destination. Is that true?"

"Yes."

"So you must admit that he lives, for the most part at least, in the past, that is to say in his past travelling experience, and that he takes no pleasure in the contemplation of the future or of his distant past. He no more knows where the track leads than I do, for all his great age. He no more knows his origins than I do, for all the fact that he is well known along the track, for mile after mile, way beyond the railway station you once thought of as the focus of your own starting point. So when I said the few words to you 'he will need to speed his way if he wishes to get there' I was only using the words allegorically. A figure of speech. An out-moded expression, derived from the things I have heard while on this track." After saying this he fell silent.

(130)

A., listening in the dark, thought that he had fallen asleep but, on hearing him stir and then sit up, he averted his gaze, and stared up at the stars. "You once said," and he might have been speaking aloud, for he was on the verge of sleep himself. "You once said that there were people you mistrusted. Men you called 'trackside philosophers'."

"Yes?" The tall man's voice showed his alertness.

"Couldn't it be argued that there was a streak of that in yourself?"

"No." The downward inflection of this negation indicated that the question had been put to him before, for this negative answer came on the tail of *A.*'s question. "No, that isn't so. I have been trying to tell the truth. It is the other people who need more scrupulous attention. You have to be careful with them. I'm speaking of all manner of men; fortune-tellers, cartomancers, tricksters of all kinds. They can look so trustworthy, and so innocent. But it's all nonsense. They may hazard a guess as to your destination, but be sure of this: they will speak with apparent certainty. I have learned this in my travels: always mistrust a man who speaks with certainty on these matters. If ever –" and he leaned over towards the younger man " – a man looks at you, and puts down his finger to stress a point, and stares you in the eyes, and makes a statement about a fact that should only be the cause of circumspect opinion, then you are looking at either a fool or an untrustworthy man who has already sized up the extent of your credulity." He paused. "I can't put it stronger," he said.

IX

The speed at which the travellers made their way along the track differed according to the nature of each traveller. The old and the enfeebled walked slowly, taking frequent breaks; sometimes they were helped by the more able travellers; sometimes, because they sought no aid, or because they independently resisted any offer of help towards their forward progress, they remained by the trackside. Other travellers, active and young, made their way rapidly, as though eager to discover what lay ahead. It often happened that travellers would stop, and make camp, and that others that they had met weeks or even months ago would thus catch them up. Then, at those rare times, old acquaintanceship would be renewed. Spirits would be proffered, and food shared. Perhaps, to the villagers who lived beneath the railway embankment, these small domestic festivals appeared crude and barbaric. These villagers would look up to the high embankment and see the flames of a fire, and hear the shouts of the travellers who danced like drunken demons in their brief merriment. And the next morning, when the villagers ventured up to the boundary wire of the railway, the ashes of the fire would be dead and the travellers gone.

There were times of merriment, certainly, but there were also deadly feuds, arguments, fights, anxieties as to the short-lived territorial rights of a traveller or a group of travellers. And, amidst the merriment and the sourness of vituperation, the card-sharps, the fortune-tellers and the wandering prognosticators flourished.

Life was an easy commodity amongst the travellers. It is difficult from our viewpoint to see the cheapness of the travellers' lives. They had lived; they had been born; they had made transient friendships and equally transient enmities. But all these things were super-ficial. All things; even the courtship between young men and young women. An absence from the camp fire – a brief shrug of the shoulders – perhaps some gesturing, or a crude joke, or a glance across the glowing gledes. Mating at least was a chance thing; a thing of circumspection when the time was judged fit; a thing of rapid dual solitude, quick penetration and impregnation.

And death was common too. A resigned figure sat by a quarter-mile post, emaciated as a corpse, but still looking to its destiny along the track. A brief and half unconscious glance from a band of travellers: does this dying man need help, or is his death something private, belonging to him alone? Will he be willing to die and, later, to be pushed down the embankment, to be buried at the expense of the parish he died in, in a corner of some graveyard, with a cross that has no name to it?

And the names of the travellers, too. How they

altered! The ease with which a traveller could change his name, depending on the company he was in; how he could be known for his considerate silence or his irritating loquacity; how he could press forward, acting as a leader in an ill-formed band, keeping his fellow travellers together and then, when depression caught him, how he would be happy to be led, drawn onward by the encouraging words of other and unrenowned men. And, next day, perhaps the same man would relinquish his identity with such a group, and travel on his own, at night, walking past the night fires and the solitary encampments. He would pass the rich and poor, the idle and the hardworking, the honest and the disloyal.

*

Autumn came, and the first breath of frost.

*

During his time of travel, A. saw his tall companion only intermittently. They had not relinquished their friendship; on the contrary, they were pleased to see each other when their paths crossed. They both walked at about the same pace along the railway, though separately, so they came across each other every other day. The fact that they travelled together no longer was merely a reflection of their different characters. Both had made other friends and, besides, the tall man had met a group of travellers, one of which included a girl who (or so he told A.) had attracted his interest. But, for all this, *A*. and the tall man were pleased to meet each other and, as their meetings became less frequent, so the two men had more to tell each other. They talked the mundane talk of the railway; the state of the food supplies; the nature of the ground over which they were travelling; superstitions they had heard of the land ahead; the watering places; the groups of other travellers whose company ought to be sought or avoided.

*

Autumn had set in by the time that *A*. left the railway. He left it not of his own volition, but strangely enough, because of the old man he had once spoken to at the side of the derelict platelayers' hut.

A. had been travelling alone all day. He regarded himself as a traveller with reason now; he wore a suit which had been given to him by a widow. This, a curious city garment with a coat of black and trousers of a pin-striped charcoal grey, fitted *A*. tolerably well. It was possibly because *A*.'s physique had reminded the widow of her own husband's that she gave the traveller the suit. And, in addition to the suit, *A*, had inherited, by proxy as it were, other articles of the dead man's clothing. The fact that he now had a suit of good clothes gave him a certain sense of vanity. One of the first things he did after he acquired that clothing was to wash himself, using the soap he had found and carefully saved. He shaved, boiling a pan of water for the purpose.

The fact that he was now dressed well, even immaculately by travellers' standards, altered his identity in the eyes of the travellers. He was now able to insinuate himself into any group; several times, at dusk, he had come unexpectedly on a band of unknown people. He had seen them stare up at him, seeing his professional appearance. He had been asked for advice on a multitude of things, most of which had their origins in the various superstitions that abounded amongst the travellers. Once he had been approached by a man younger than himself, scarcely a youth. This youth, a pale boy with fair hair, had come up to him so timidly that at first *A.* thought that he might have had some nefarious purpose in mind. But that was not so. The boy had asked him the distance to a certain place.

"What place is that?"

"They tell me that it lies along the line of the railway."

"Which way?" *A.* stood in the centre of the track, pointing in either direction. He looked down at the boy.

"Forwards." The boy nodded in the direction of the hills, which at that time they had almost reached.

"I've not been there." *A.* was frank in his answer. He had heard too many bluffs and blusters in his time to tell such a lie himself. "I don't know what lies ahead. Of course, you hear all kinds of things here on the railway." He checked himself. He was aware that he was speaking as the tall man might speak, his words uncertain circumlocutions. "No, I don't know."

(136)

"They tell me the terminus is there," said the boy.

A. looked at him closely. There seemed to be no guile in the boy; his face was honest and open. He had spoken with some urgency.

"How long have you been travelling?" asked *A.*

"I was born on the railway," said the boy.

"I ought to have guessed that."*A.* paused, partly for breath; he had been walking with exceptional rapidity. Now he started to walk again. The boy trotted at his side, nervously active, not breathless in any way.*A.* had begun to realise the rapidity and the earnestness which those who had been born on the railway possessed. He pointed to the hills. "Who told you there was the terminus of the railway there?"

The boy looked up at him, grinning. Apparently he found this rapid pace agreeable; he was much more at his ease now than when he had been standing.

A., somewhat to his own discomfort, began to break into a run also. He had no idea why he was doing this. All he knew was that the faster he ran the more at ease the boy at his side became. The fact that his question was unanswered did not bother him, at least for the time being; it took all his energy to keep pace with the boy.

After a mile he was unable to run any further. He paused, halting for breath. He stopped. The track was exactly the same. He might have achieved no distance whatsoever. The boy, pausing ahead of him, looked regretfully back at him, surprised that he should be out of breath and, briefly looking back, he began to run on ahead at a steady pace.

A., sitting down at the side of the track on a fallen telegraph pole, watched the youthful figure as it receded into distance. Although he could see that the boy was running fast – much faster than he had been when he had been accompanying *A.* at an easy jogging pace – it took several minutes, or perhaps almost quarter of an hour, for him to disappear from view, hidden by the small trees that had sprung from the railway bed.

A. rested for no longer than he wished, for the urge to be on his way soon overcame him again. He continued his walking, his gaze cast down at the moving track before his feet.

He came across the old man. It was inevitable that he should; the old man sat under a roofless hut, a platelayers' hut, identical to many such buildings regularly placed along the track-side. This hut was in no way different, except that it had a rotten upper storey, made of wood. The slates had gone from this, and most of the roof. A single gable with a corroded iron finial pointed up at the sky. A rotten wooden platform indicated that the place might once have been a halt.

A. looked at the building and, seeking a place to stay the night, he saw the old man's meagre fire before he saw the old man himself. He had not expected to see the old man; he had thought that he must have left him far behind, for he had been travelling rapidly, and the old man with his disabling frailty could hardly have overtaken him. For all that, however, the facts were there. Here sat the old man. He sat against the stonework, looking down at his fire. *A.* approached him. "Do you remember me?"

The old man looked up. There was no element of recognition in his face. He stared at *A.*, and then his gaze drifted down to his fire. *A.* found this somewhat perplexing; previously, when he had seen the old man, the ancient's stare had been penetrating and universal. Now the old man stared down at the ground where he sat. When he spoke it was to utter nonsense. "Are you another of them?"

"Another of them? What do you mean?"

The old man did not look up. He behaved as though he had not heard *A.*'s words. Yet, apparently, he had heard other sounds; when, for instance, a sound of a shotgun echoed from the hills he turned his head. The fact that he could hear, but had not hear *A.*'s words, made the young man suddenly afraid. "What do you mean?" *A.* repeated.

The old man put out his hands and curved his shoulders, in order to gain the heat from the fire. *A.* saw the emaciated hands and the thin wrists. Now they were almost skeletal.

"Do you want some food?" *A.* began to withdraw a package from his pocket. "Something to drink?"

The old man still made no recognition of hearing *A.*'s voice. He crouched closer to the fire, and the smoke brushed through the fingers of his hands. When he looked up his eyes were watering profusely. He looked at *A.* He opened his mouth to speak, but no words were uttered.

"What is it?" *A*. knelt in front of the old man.

"There was a boy here, some time ago. Perhaps half an hour. Perhaps longer. Who can tell? He was born on the railway, here. You know it. You know these things. It's a fact you recognise." The words were slow in coming. "I'm prevaricating," said the old man. He looked at *A*.'s clothes. For the first time he showed a certain degree of interest. He put out a hand and touched the black jacket, and touched the hem of the grey trousers. He looked at the material closely. "Are you a lawyer too?" he asked. "I was a lawyer. It was a long time ago. I have seen you before, haven't I? You weren't in lawyers' clothes then."

A., who had not been aware that for the last two days he had been wearing dress appropriate to a lawyer, shook his head. "No. They were given to me," he said.

Again the old man gave no impression of having heard. He leaned back from the fire, and took his hands away also. He put his hands to his chest, and sat looking at the fire which was rapidly losing its heat. While he did this he kept his hand on the hem of *A*.'s coat, as though it had the power to give him a distant and half forgotten security. "There was a boy here," he said again. "He said something about a terminus."

"Yes, he mentioned that to me." *A*. reached out a hand; he saw the buttons of his own coat sleeve glimmer in the light of the dying fire. "I think you ought to rest. Have a drink of this."

The old man looked at the proffered brandy flask. He smiled, his face wrinkled. His sudden smile was the first expression that *A*. had seen in that old and wrinkled face and, aware that he was being closely observed, the old man allowed his smile to fade. He took the bottle. "Once," he said, "I was at a revival camp meeting, on the roadside, a long way the other side of your city. I was a child then, from a traveller's point of view, though I was a qualified and registered lawyer. That's the difference. One's qualifications count for nothing on the track here. Once I came upon a revival sect. They blocked the way. They were standing on a wooden stand, talking about the evil of alcohol. One man, I remember, a large man in a frock coat and long hair, held up a bottle of plum spirit, or it might have been brandy. He poured some into a spoon and ignited it. He told us that the blue flames were like the brimstone flames of hell. He took a glass and poured into it a good measure of the spirit, and then one of his helpers – a young woman, grey and flat chested – handed him up a cardboard box and a saucer. He opened the box. We all peered into the box because he opened it so gingerly. We were eager to find out what was in it. In fact it was no more than a small frog, a little leaping thing the size of a coin. He held it up, smiling. He dropped the frog into the glass and we saw it struggle as it died; he had covered up the glass with the saucer. He passed the box back to the woman. Then he dipped finger and thumb into the glass, and pulled out the frog, holding it by its hind leg, so that it dangled down. He shouted temperance at us for an hour, holding up the frog before he threw it down the track. Flecks of spit had formed at the corners of his mouth.

"Such was his rhetoric, such was his power of speaking, his hypnotism, his talking voice, that when the papers with the pledge went round we all signed, me amongst the rest of them, and I am a lawyer too. That's what qualifications mean, when you are lonely; lonely on the track, with nothing to do but listen to a hypnotic bigot." As he was saying this, in a slow dry monotone, he was staring into the depths of the bottle. Speedily he raised it up, saluting *A*. "Here goes," he said.

He passed the bottle back to *A*., who recorked it and put it back in his pocket.

A. decided to stay the night with the old man. He stood up, looking up and down the track. The night was surprisingly warm for the time of year. Careful of his new jacket, he hung it from a low porcelain insulator which still jutted from an iron bracket set in the masonry of that shell of a hut. He put on the greatcoat, also part of his inherited wardrobe, a handsome coat, of full city length, with wide fur lapels and double-breasted with a wide belt. He lay down beside the fire, opposite the old man. He adjusted his pack under his head.

He was drifting off to sleep when he heard the old man mutter something. He could not catch the words and, when he sleepily asked the old man to repeat what he had said, he knew that he would receive no reply, for the old man himself was asleep.

A. looked at him. The old man certainly chose an odd posture in which to sleep, leaning against a wall. His coat was not even buttoned. *A*. crawled over to him, and buttoned the coat. The old man did not move. His breathing was slow and quiet.

The night passed dreamlessly, and the two of them were undisturbed, though many travellers must have passed them by, for the railway was, at that time, crowded with journeying travellers.

*

A. woke early in the morning, aroused by the crowing of a cock. He lay in half sleep. There was the sound as of a distant turmoil. Not far away a tower clock struck the hour of six.

He raised himself up, stiff with cold, and half drugged with sleep. He looked down the embankment and saw that, obscured by a light but clinging mist, a town lay beneath them. Evidently they had camped not far from a bridge that spanned an arterial road.

A. stood fully, taking in the extent of the town. It was small, as far as he could see, but the mist precluded his further vision. A parish church stood at the end of a green. On each side of it were two public houses, jutting their signs out into the street. One of these signs portrayed a bell; the other a swan. Two rows of houses ran down the side of the street to the railway.

A. looked at the old man, and saw that he was still asleep. *A*. let him sleep on. He reached up for his coat which still hung from the insulator. He took off his greatcoat, and put on the city lawyer's coat. Only then did he remember that the old man had not been asleep. A seasoned traveller now, *A*. knew death when he saw it. He bent down and touched the old face and he knew before he touched it that the old face would be cold. A fine dew, borne of the thin mist, lay on the bald scalp and the white cheekbones.

A. looked about him. He was tempted for a moment to walk on, and leave the parishioners of this town to look after the old man and see to his burial. This, however, he found impossible. He gathered the old man's few belongings together, and put them in his pocket. He picked up the old man as a man might pick up a child. There was no weight to the body. Then, half bending to pick up his own pack as well, he walked down a flight of steps that led from the disused halt to the town.

*

In the town below it was not so much the fact that a corpse had been brought down from the railway, for that was a mundane thing; the surprise was that the corpse was carried by a young man, evidently a city lawyer from his dress. *A.* had indeed kept good care of his inherited suit of clothes; now, as he carried the body of the old man, he looked quite unlike a vagrant; indeed, there was an air of prosperity about him. The townspeople who saw him were not to know that the shrewdness of his face was due to trial, imprisonment and long travelling; perhaps they mistook his expression for the intelligent expression of a good advocate, or even the judicial expression of a judge.

It was thus that, his identity mistaken, *A.* was relieved of the corpse without questioning. The body of the old man was taken to the west door of the parish church, where a poor man's bier would await it. *A.* was led to the larger and more prosperous of the two inns, where he met the landlord, a thin and active little man of no great age. This landlord, who had seen or been told about *A.*'s arrival at the town, showed him into a back room and gave him a glass of brandy, *gratis*, perhaps feeling that a lawyer might be expected to be out of sorts after carrying a corpse down from the railway: alternatively the man might have given *A.* the drink in order to secure his patronage for the duration of his stay in the town.

A. put his case and the few belongings of the old man on a chair at his side. He patted his pockets, smoothing his coat; he remembered that he had picked up and put in his own pockets various other belongings of the old man. He sat down and began to examine them. He discovered a wallet which held banknotes of a denomination unknown to him; on the back of these notes was engraved a picture of an unknown tower, while on the front was a portrait of an unknown lord, or king, or prelate. He studied the banknotes for a minute or more. The depicted nobleman appeared to have some priestly function, for in addition to a crown he wore a stole, and there was an episcopal coat of arms above his crown. Perhaps *A.* was looking at the picture of a prince-bishop of some very distant town, way beyond his own city. He turned the notes over. They were, he noticed, crudely engraved, as though very old; they did not have any serial number on them. He folded them and put them back in the wallet. The only other thing he found in the wallet was a small sepia photograph of a group, perhaps the old man's own family. The old man had never spoken of his family. A tall young man stood by the side of a sitting woman. Their studied posture and the foxing of the photograph showed that the thing was ancient. Perhaps the old man had been no more than *A.*'s age at the instant of the photograph; perhaps the sitting woman had been his wife. Perhaps the house in the background had been his house.

A. began to drink his brandy.

He had laid down his glass again in order to look at various other things that had belonged to the old man, when the door opened and four men entered. *A.* began to half stand; he thought he recognised three of them, for there was a kind of unity in their expression and in the direction of their gaze. He was reminded immediately of the three men who had stood on the top floor of a distant town hall, many miles away. The fourth figure, the man who had entered first, could have been the magistrate of the same town, but *A.* had no chance to see him properly; now the man walked round a pillar and sat in a chair where his face was invisible. *A.* was forced to stand up and walk a little to one side in order to observe the newcomer's face; he did this and found the man staring back at him. There was no sign of recognition; this sitting man was not the magistrate of that distant town, although there was a superficial resemblance. This stranger now gazed up at *A.*, perhaps wondering why he was being stared at.

After looking at *A.* speculatively for a few moments, obviously taking the stock of the young man in the lawyer's clothes, he stood up and walked over to *A.* "I apologise if I intrude," he said, his voice friendly, considering he had never met *A.* before, "but I seem to recognise you. And you, I thought, seemed to recognise me."

"No, I was mistaken," said *A.* "I thought at first that you resembled the magistrate at a distant town. That was all."

"Oh." The newcomer was obviously flattered, or that was the reaction he gave, though it could have only been surprise. "What was the name of the town?"

"I don't remember that," said *A.*, quite honestly. Since his journeying had started he had passed through so many towns that he had difficulty in remembering any of them clearly. And besides, the station nameboards still stood at nearly every station and halt, and as there had been halts at very regular distances, perhaps every mile or so, a profusion of names had offered themselves for recall. "No, I've travelled through so many towns that I can't remember."

The newcomer looked at *A.*'s legal dress; it must have been unusual to see such formality in a little town like this. "Are you on a court circuit?" he asked.

A. looked up at the man. "No," he said. "I am only travelling." For a moment he wished to tell this stranger that he was not a lawyer, that his clothes had been inherited. But he dismissed this thought. While travelling he had heard so many life histories that he found them to hold the same elements of fact and fiction as his own. He had no wish to repeat other men's tales.

The other man was asking him a question. "Where are you going?" He drew up a chair beside A. The other three men remained at the other end of the room, from which they stared in the direction of the newcomer, or at A., or, perhaps, merely in that general direction. Their stare began to make A. feel a little faint. He was reminded of the tall man and his superstition about the pursuers from the town. Perhaps his very words, recalled now by A., acted on his mind and made him feel faint. He took a drink from his glass.

He looked at the newcomer, who was waiting, in a tolerant and complacent manner, for a reply. A. looked at him, about to speak, but acutely aware of the presence of the three men at the other end of the room.

"Now I know I'm being intrusive!" said the newcomer, at ease now. Perhaps A.'s reticence had been enough to give him away as being a traveller along the railway. At all events, the newcomer leaned back in his chair, looking sideways at A. "Do you know this part of the country well?" he asked, although only a few seconds ago he had admitted that he had been intrusive.

"No. I know it hardly at all." A. faced him. "I have been travelling along the railway."

"Oh, yes, yes, I saw that," said the newcomer. "There was no mistaking that at all." There was a passing irritation in his voice, as though his observational shrewdness had been questioned. "It's only that

(148)

your action and your manners and even your dress are, well, frankly at odds with those of a traveller. I –" and he threw out his hands " – avoid the term 'vagrant' because one occasionally meets people like yourself who, superficially at least, seem to have a great deal of purpose in what they do. Or so it seems. That was why I came in here. They told me you had arrived and I wanted to see you, informally, here, rather than in the Magistrate's Rooms, which are rather less informal and, I might say, are less pleasant also. I like to talk to those of the travellers who stray into the town from the railway."

"You are the Magistrate here then?"

"Yes; in fact, I am a Magistrate Surrogate, to be truthful. But that is by the way." He summoned the landlord and ordered something to drink, and told the man to fill A.'s glass. "I think that this parish has something of a reputation amongst the travellers."

"Why should that be?"

"We try to keep a close census of those who pass through our town, on the railway. It's nothing formal. You may have seen a few men standing on some of the overbridges, looking down. They try to keep a record of all who pass into the parish, noting down the times, and various descriptions of them. We take a similar tally of those who pass along the railway, when they leave our parish. In this way we can get reasonably accurate figures, not only of the numbers of people who have passed, but also of projected figures. In fact, the number of people passing along the railway has increased almost exponentially in the last few years.

Our projections show (though of course one can but hope the trend will tail off) that in ten years' time the railway will be so full of people that there will be hardly a yard between them. We find this worrying in the extreme.

"When I first came here, I thought that this record-keeping was a useless exercise, quite a waste of time, as I can see you do, at least to judge by your expression. But it isn't so. The increasing number of people travelling along the railway is giving us great cause for concern. As I have said, numbers have increased beyond reason in the last few years. Now, we here in this parish feel some responsibility towards those who travel. It's difficult not to feel some emotion towards them. At one time, a few years ago, it was mooted by the parish council that the bridge should be dismantled, thus blocking off the railway. A number of other parishes have thought the same thing. This idea came to nothing, here as elsewhere, because all that would do would be to create a great unmoving mass of people at the railway's end. And, of course, they are resourceful people; they would span the broken arch, or even come down into the town. So we left the bridge intact, thinking that that would create less suffering, on balance.

"It was when I heard that you, a lawyer, were seen travelling along the railway that I thought I ought to seek you out, and find out more about what is happening in other parishes, how they are dealing with the problem, how things are managed. And, if possible, to find out why people are travelling along the railway at all; after all, it is still private property. Since the bankruptcy of the Eastern Provincial Railway Company, the land has all reverted to the original parishes through which it once ran.

"These are the things that I wanted to ask. For that reason I hoped that you would come down from the railway. I never thought that the thing that would bring you down here would have been that humanitarian and selfless act of carrying a dead man. He was no relation of yours?"

"No."

The Magistrate dismissed the thought of the dead man. He beckoned for his three clerks to join them at the table. One of these men opened a small case and brought out various documents, which he laid in front of the Magistrate.

The Magistrate took up one of these papers, a large chart showing the numbers of people who had passed through the parish. This data was correlated with the month of the year, and with past years. Projections had been made into the future. The number of deaths while in the parish had been recorded, and the male to female ratio of the travellers, and the estimated age of the travellers. The surface of the table soon became a mass of papers, all showing various things; truth, speculation, even fictional hypotheses, represented by bar-charts, histograms, cluster charts, graphs and other less easily understood documents. One of the clerks muttered something in a statistical jargon and *A.* caught the phrases 'analysis of variance' and 'row and column effects'. Another clerk produced a pocket calculator, the panel of which glowed with green light and flickering figures.

The result of this effort meant nothing to *A*. He had never been particularly numerate; now he was being shown things that meant nothing to him. He knew that in a moment's time his opinion would be sought. The Magistrate had meanwhile fallen into a brief and arid argument with his demographic clerk about some trivial detail. His long finger jabbed down on a piece of paper where the average speed of travelling the three miles of the parish had been recorded for several thousand travellers. Perhaps he was pointing out some inaccuracy. The demographic clerk was staring at his calculator. "We could do that, sir, but I hardly think it was in our brief." He looked down at the Magistrate, his manner that of a man who shows as much open dislike to his superior as he dares. "No, it was hardly in our original brief." "Then you ought to have taken the initiative," said the Magistrate wearily. He pointed to a cross-hatched section of the histogram. The clerk was unconvinced. "Very well, then. If you wish." He pressed the buttons of his calculator in rapid succession and read out a figure that meant nothing to *A*., though it seemed to mollify the Magistrate.

The Magistrate turned to *A*. "Do you see our problem?"

"Yes, I can see you have a problem," said *A*. "Perhaps you might try to find out its exact nature before you attempt to solve it."

The Magistrate looked at *A*. in an irritated manner, then, possibly remembering that *A*. was not in his employ, he leaned back. "Perhaps you are right though. Perhaps we have gone about things the wrong way." He turned to the officer who was muttering something in his ear. He nodded, vigorously. He pulled out a piece of paper. "So many things have been documented that it's difficult to judge the accuracy of the end result," he said. "Perhaps the data could be analysed differently, though I have to say that our results have taken any observational error into account."

A. suddenly remembered that he had seen some watchers on a bridge, near a wayside halt. He remembered that he had been travelling by night. The watchers, standing round a brazier, had been warming their hands and passing a bottle round. *A.* knew that he had not been observed. He glanced down at the sea of papers in front of him. He allowed himself a smile. If the data had been collected by such careless and unvigilant observers, what could the accurately computed projections mean? He turned to the Magistrate. "Your problem is one of observational error," he said.

"Nonsense!" The Magistrate showed the signs of anger at this. "What do you mean by that?"

"If you were to travel along the railway yourself, at night, you would see what kind of watch they keep."

"I? Are you suggesting that I travel along the railway? And at night?" He paled, as if the thought were distasteful or repugnant. He looked at his three clerks. They said nothing, but stared woodenly at *A.*

A. stood up. He was no longer afraid of the clerks' stare, nor of the close proximity of the Magistrate. He had realised the inanity of what they had set out to do,

(153)

and the way in which they had done it. Besides, there was something of a personal affront in the fact that he might have been labelled as a cipher amongst innumerable ciphers in their inaccurate statistics. He began to walk to the door.

"Where are you going?" The Magistrate had stood.

"Back to the railway."

"So you will not help us?"

"How can I help? I have offered what I could as a traveller, and you were angry after my first few words. In that light how may I continue?"

The Magistrate called for the landlord. He turned to A. "At least you'll take lunch with us here."

"I must be on my way."

The Magistrate had crossed the room. He grasped A. by an elbow. "What drives you on? Where are you going? Or are you escaping?"

A. smiled wearily. "Those are dramatic questions. And they are old. I cannot answer them."

"But you must. If not for your own sake, then for the sake of other travellers on the railway. Remember that from these statistics we might be able to gauge what sort of sustenance we could be expected to give the travellers. We distribute food in the winter, from the platform of the old station. We attempt to see to their needs: soup, and potatoes, and bread; and what clothing we can offer. But we need these statistics to judge the amount of stores to get in; the number of auxiliary gravediggers too, for when the winter sets in."

By saying these things he had put a doubt in A.'s mind. A. thought back to the other magistrate; the difference between the two men was so great that it seemed strange that they should hold the same parochial post. He thought of the peculiarly local conclusions which this man had made from other men's cursory and erratic observations. For a moment he wondered whether the conclusions he had made in his youth had been founded on equally cursory premises. He shook his hand free. "I can give you a guess," he said. "You'll need as much food as you can get and as much grave space as you can spare. You can't do more than that. How can you expect me to say anything else? Why don't you take each event as it comes? You can only influence a life when it comes under the jurisdiction of your parish." He said this as though he had intended to speak for effect. He might have said more had he not been distracted by the smells of the kitchen. The landlord had left the kitchen door open.

A. glanced at the Magistrate and, beyond him, at the three clerks who were replacing their documents in the case. The tallest of the three clerks was tapping out something on his calculator. *A.* looked across at him. The man held the thing away from himself so that the green panel could adventitiously be seen by *A.* The arbitrary number for some reason fixed itself in *A.*'s memory, for the fluorescent green was totally at variance with any other colour in the room. The number was 999, but, as *A.* reflected later, the man might have been holding the calculator upside down.

He looked away from the calculator as the clerk switched it off. "Yes, I'll stay to lunch with you," he said.

X

A. stood, a man in a ragged line, underneath the canopy of a wayside railway station. He had kept no reckoning of the miles but the track might have been endless, so straight was it. And now he was here, at a wayside station, waiting for a wayfarer's dole of soup and bread and, with luck, some ale. He stood in the line, tenth in that line. In front of him was an old man who might have been the brother of the old lawyer. Behind him was a young family, led by a husband younger than *A.*, a wolfish young man who *A.* had at first avoided because of his reputation. However, *A.* had grown to forgive him, for the young man was only acting on behalf of his family. Three nights ago *A.* had sat with them, this family, and had shared their fire and their food, distributing his own food amongst the children. By doing this he had been accepted amongst them, a vicarious uncle to the children. But the scene here was the usual one; the queue of people, indifferent and silent. The day might have been any other. The nameboard of the station stood on its two poles, but the name was unimportant. Under the circumstances the fact that the canopy of the station was now entirely vestigial, for all its glazing was gone, was more important. It afforded no protection against the elements now; snow fell through its unglazed metalwork.

And as for the travellers? They had altered with the coming of winter too. Now even the most gracile amongst them was a dark soot-black smudge, hesitantly makings its way through the snow, watchful of craters and potholes. The land on either side was covered by a frozen flood and the grey sky portended more snow. They had changed with the weather, visually, but beyond that they were the same travellers though the weather had altered them. The talkative had grown silent; the loquacious avoided empty talk. The newcomers to the railway still asked the usual questions; the old superstitions were still given, in a whispering undertone, from frozen mouth to freezing ear. Goods were passed on from dying to living, and the quick stole from the dead.

With the soup and charity ale warm within him, *A.* wandered down the track, a lump of bread in his hands. He still had a store of food with him, and he would attempt to use the bread he held to secure the confidence of the family he had latched on to. It was said, it had been told him, that true loneliness came in winter on the railway. He looked back.

He looked back, and the scene was worth the looking at. It could have been used as a model by some romantic painter, but there was no romanticism there. The redundant station stood silent, its finials white against the grey sky. The glassless canopy allowed the snow to fall on the heads of the plump town matrons who doled out the charity food. The light from the field stoves illuminated the trampled snow of the platform.

The hour of charity over, the saucepans empty, the townswomen were preparing to depart. A group of men from the town, dressed in long grey fleeces, apparently a traditional winter dress in this area, were laughing and passing round a bottle of spirits preparatory to venturing up the track to look for the bodies of the fallen. They pushed through the waiting crowd of travellers, who allowed them to pass with a sullen silence. The situation could have been tense; a fist raised, and the hostility of the town would have overcome its worn generosity.

*

The night had set in early. The family camped under a railway arch, huddled close to the small fire. A. had been allowed to join the family though he sat somewhat apart. The young man, the husband, had gone down to the plain to find what he could. Before he left he had talked to A. for some while, a rare event, for he was a habitually silent man. His wife and children had been asleep.

*

"Where do you come from?" This was the first direct question that the husband had asked. His eyes were suspicious and his gaze concentrated, so much so that the man he was talking to was reminded of the stare of the tall man who had once been his travelling companion.

"I came from the city."

The wolfish man nodded his head. The answer was enough. "I've heard of it. But I have passed through so many towns that I forget the name of the place. I was only born there. My parents were on the track a week afterwards. It was winter then too, they tell me." He grinned, unexpectedly. *A.* had never seen any emotion in him before. "It could be my birthday," he said. He brought out a flask that *A.* had never known that he had possessed. "Here."

"Thank you." *A.* took a drink from the flask. The spirit was strange, strong, and perhaps locally distilled; it had a faint taste of almonds under its fiery spirituousness.

"Tell me," said the young man, "why you have been so good to us." He smiled again as he took back the flask. He drank. "I've noticed it, many times. You have been saving food, giving it to my wife for the children. Why?" He shrugged his shoulders. "Perhaps one should not question these things, but it's strange. I was suspicious of you at first. Did you know that?"

"You are suspicious of every man who you meet," said *A.* "You're a man with a clear head, and a fighter. You put your family before everything else. Perhaps I shouldn't say these things, either. The travellers keep clear of you, as you probably know. They say you killed a man once, in a town, in a fight. I forget who told me that."

"Yes, it was true. Last year. We were down in the plain, and they caught us in the fields. They were stupid; they wouldn't listen to what we had to say. Big, brave boys, wanting to show their strength. They went down like pancakes in the fight. You are right. One was killed. I might have done it." He looked down at his gloved hands and, as though feeling the cold, he removed the gloves and held his hands close to the fire. His hands were large and square, and his nails were longer than the nails of the usual traveller.

A. began to wonder about his ancestry. "You asked me why I had saved food for your children," said *A.*

"That's it. I'm not above being suspicious now."

"The straight answer is that I hesitated to go on alone. It is said that the railway is best wintered in company."

The young man stared at him, disbelieving. "That's not true. I heard the opposite. I heard that it was each man for himself in winter," he said. "But who knows the truth of it? It all depends on who we are, and on where we are going.

"Have you noticed how things have changed? Not as regards landscape, or weather, or season, but how the railway changes, as you get on? It's a strange thing." He leaned forward, perhaps ashamed at being so unusually talkative. "I don't want to raise all the old superstitions," he said. "But you must have seen this happening."

"No, I'm not quite sure what you mean," said *A.*

The young man shot him a faintly suspicious glance before passing over the flask again. "The further you travel, and the further you go, the greater is the dominance of the railway. Perhaps that's why I, being born on it, almost, and you have such different approaches."

"How did you meet your wife?"

"On the railway. She belonged to a larger family than mine; I suppose we've left them far behind now, if they are still alive. They were against us going together. But it was inevitable. An itinerant preacher with an eye for propriety married us when she was pregnant. He was a strange old man. He travelled with us for some time. I was never sure as to which sect he belonged to; perhaps he was confused over that himself. I can remember his little marriage ceremony though, as if it had been yesterday. Winter, as now. Half the marriage was in some foreign language, but it seemed to put things in order then, not that it matters much now." He looked down at his family. "I've been meaning to say this to you for some time."

A. listened; he knew what the man would say. He knew that he would be asked to look after the survivors of the winter, should anything happen to either husband or wife.

But the husband did not put it quite like that. He was diffident, feeling his independence strongly. He was straightforward in his speaking, in the habit of a silent man saying something he earnestly wishes to communicate. He leaned back against the stonework of the bridge. "I hate their superstitions," he was saying, "but I have a feeling that I have seen this land before and, whether you know it or not, that's reckoned an ill omen. As I say, about the superstitions and all that – you can forget it. But it has struck me once or twice. I seem to remember standing under that railway station canopy. I don't know what made me think of it, but I thought I had seen the place before. Perhaps I was mistaken; certainly I was. I have always walked in the same direction, as do we all. And there was another time –" He paused. "What does it matter? What does any of it matter? All I ask is what you'd expect me to ask. I'll admit that I was wrong when I said it was better to be a lone wolf in winter. You were right." He smiled slightly. "What made you say that? Had you heard it said, or did you think of it? The fact that it has to be better, travelling in company, in the winter?"

A. shook his head. "I'm not sure. It's often difficult, or it seems difficult, to tell the difference between fact and fable, or between what you know and what you have been told; I can't remember where I heard that one."

"It's true. There are no origins in these things." He passed the flask over again. "Have some more. My birthday." He gazed at *A.* as though he had found a fast friend, a rare event for a man with a family.

"They say," muttered *A.*, "about you that you have a number of habits that don't tie in with your being born on the railway."

"What are they?" The young man spoke with a silent humour.

"They say that you find women down in the towns. That you are well known for that. But, from the care you take, I can't believe that you are unfaithful."

"I have never been unfaithful to my wife," said the young man. "And as for the other women –" He shrugged his shoulders. He smiled slightly. "They

(162)

know who and what they're getting. They know that I must be on my way; that I can never stop; the women are the same with all travellers. Their towns are there. The women want something they know will never last.

"Of course they do. That's the attraction of a traveller for them. You must have seen them yourself, standing by the track, unless you don't see these things, or unless you aren't interested. In summer and spring, of course, the traditional seasons. They summon you with their tight blouses. It's all a question of a fleeting lust and a fleeting love. They're faithful too, to what they know and the things they understand."

"But you contradict yourself," said *A*. "You would never let another man touch your wife. You know it. Earlier you asked me to look after your family if anything happened to you. Very well. You know my answer. But I would be only a guardian. I'd fear your ghost if I entertained any thoughts about your wife. You have a reputation." Delivered in a half serious and half jocular manner, this speech made the young man laugh.

"Don't fear my ghost," he said. "Just make sure I am dead before you touch her."

*

Winter progressed, and walking was difficult. The husband and wife and *A*. each carried a child, and *A*. knew that he had been accepted into the family for the duration of the winter. And, as the winter progressed, so their pace slowed. And, with the slowing pace, so

(163)

the travellers increased in number. Fuel was scarce, buried under snow. Means of making fire were at a premium, and a man with a petrol lighter was a friend to be fed for an evening.

One afternoon they were walking along, carefully. The tracks in the snow had been obliterated by a fresh fall, and the trees at the trackside's edge were black and brittle. The track ran on, through hills, straight as a ruled line over viaduct and through deep cutting. They made unusually good progress that afternoon, unless, as had happened before, the varied terrain of the country through which they were passing made the miles seem short.

The track ran through a small range of hills, where, beyond, must run a great valley.

A. had noticed something strange about the rock formations above the railway cutting through which they were walking. He looked up; the child on his shoulders felt his disquiet. He walked on. He had been telling the child a story, but the configuration of that high rock formation stayed with him in memory, and he looked back. He looked back and he saw the serrated skyline. His heart beat more rapidly, and he was aware of the cold. The child he carried began to cry.

Both husband and wife turned back at the sound.

To *A.* there was something startling about the intensity of their gaze; the stare from fixed and cold faces. They stood, husband and wife, in the railway cutting, both figures enframed by an overarching bridge.

"Alexander, what is the matter?" The young man's wife began to run back; her face was distressed; *A.* wondered what he must look like for his face to have provoked this reaction in her. He shook his head.

"You look bewildered; what is the matter?" She put an ungloved hand to his face. The young man watched from the middle distance, trying to size up the situation.

A. looked about him. "I know this place," he said.

He knew this place. He knew the high rock formation he had scaled as a boy. He had looked down then at the railway track.

He knew where he was, and the thought was too much for the mind to bear. He looked at the low range of hills. He saw the cutting. He knew that, a half mile hence, the high and rocky ridge would fall to a valley where a city lay, filled with towers, where the railway spanned that valley with a great viaduct.

He put down the crying child and ran on. He ran to the young man, stopping for a moment.

"You are as white as a sheet."

"I know this place. I know it full well."

The young man caught his arm. "Stop; that's only a superstition. I remember the other night, when we were talking, I told you that I felt a familiarity with this place too. It's nothing to worry about. It can't be true."

"I know this place!" His words were exclamatory. He shook himself free of the young man's tight grip. He knew that, by the very superstitions that the railway and its travellers possessed, he would be left alone now. His very tone showed that there was nothing he wanted more than to be left by himself. After all, such things were not uncommon.

Half a mile more, and he looked down.

The snowladen city was beneath him. The viaduct was in front of him. The bells of the cathedral were booming out, and the bells of the towers of the other churches. The viaduct was overgrown and he made no attempt to walk along it; it would have been impossible for him anyway, although he could see the end of the viaduct ahead, and the beginning of the dank cutting. He took a step back, towards the long snaking road that led down to the city. It was impossible for him to summon the energy to cross the viaduct. He was exhausted.

He sat on the parapet, not bothering to brush away the snow. Way back, down the track, he could see the young man and his family; black dots, only apparent because of the contrast between their dark clothes and the pristine snow.

The sound of the bells shook the snow from the steeples, and the weather-vanes lanced the air.

Three men in the uniform of the city were walking along the viaduct towards him, over the snow. Now and then one of them would look down over the parapet, unsure of himself in this giddy height, but these acts were merely digressions: they had seen *A.* and their stare, as they approached him, became fixed upon him in recognition.

XI

A. allowed himself to be led through the streets of the
city. He, born in the city, knew the most direct way
from the base of the road that led down from the
viaduct to the law courts and the prison, and he was
surprised to find that the officer of the guard did not
take that route. The journey should have been short,
and A. had so many things to dwell upon in his mind
that he scarcely noticed the direction in which they
travelled. The sudden fact of his recognition of the
city, and his sudden forced descent into it from the
height of the viaduct, and the fact that he was being
forcibly marched, presumably to the prison, all com-
bined to make him afraid and indecisive. Yet if there
was one thing that restored his confidence in himself it
was the behaviour of the three guards themselves who,
although speaking rarely to one another and never to A.,
seemed unsure of their way. This might have been
accounted for by the fact that it was difficult to tell
which of them was the officer; he had no marks of
superior rank and his manner was the same as the
other two men. In fact, the three men were all so very
much alike that A. found himself wondering which of
them was in fact the officer, for at one moment one
man would give an order and the other two would

obey, while, some time later, another might give the order. This was difficult to prove because of their similarity. They were all three of them men in late middle age, or older, and *A*. found this fact surprising, for he had remembered his pursuers as being young, with young men's affectations of long upcurling moustaches. Now they crossed the centre of the city, where the bell for evensong had left the air shuddering with sound. *A*. suddenly found himself wondering where these three men were going. Their journey up to now had been aimless, or so it had seemed.

A. eventually spoke to one of them, a thing that he found distasteful for he had, on his journeyings, often wondered what would happen on his return to the city. He had imagined the new trial; he had learned from the old. He had expected to be marched to the prison, or at least kept under house arrest in his mother's home, though he had not seriously entertained the latter thought. He knew the fact of the coming trial.

Now he found himself in the company of three men who must have passed their retiring age. Becoming angry he turned to the man who had seemed to be the officer. "Where are we going? The law courts?"

The man looked at one of his colleagues and then accusingly back at *A*. as if to tell him that he had spoken to the wrong man.

"It's very likely that we're going past the law courts," said the second man.

A. shook himself. He was growing cold; they had been standing still for some time. "Do you know how to get there?"

"We have the official route," said the officer. "But if you know of a quicker way, you might tell us."

A. directed them. This scene of indecision had somehow made him buoyant, and he was pleased to point out the street names, at which the officer looked uncomprehendingly. They took the direct way at *A.*'s own prompting.

Once they passed the preceptorial college as the robed men came out of one of the city church portals. The arresting party, with *A.* at its centre, was about to intercept the long gaggle of old men in their red and blue robes, who struggled across the snowbound square to their college buildings. Their skinny, stockinged legs stood out like sticks against the muddy city snow. Their very decrepitude (both as individuals and in formation) seemed to point to the decrepitude of the system under which they worked and under which the city laboured. The fact that this long line of struggling old men was intercepted and broken up by the automaton-like progress of the arresting party could do nothing but hearten *A.*

He knew the system under which the court would operate. At his last trial he had been young, inexperienced, susceptible, inarticulate. Now, after his travels, he had not only learned the correct manner in which to deal with the sterile hierarchy of the city, but had planned cogent arguments to the questions that would be asked him. He even began to feel elated; his experiences would be and could be condensed to a reasoning that could easily be given without any recourse to a city advocate.

At his direction they entered the gatehouse of the building where, from a high window, a trumpeter in uniform was about to sound a reasonless curfew.

*

They walked the long corridor to the prison. This corridor backed onto a law court; it was suddenly familiar. The panelled walls, the high perspectives, the regular doors; all these things were familiar.

A figure emerged from one of the doors, opening it briefly before closing it again. He stood in front of the arresting party, but he had not seen it yet; the door had been constructed so that it looked down the corridor, and not into the open street. But A. remembered both the door and the man. The door, during the brief interval of opening in order to allow the Prosecutor egress, had also allowed the exit of both noise and smell, both of which indicated a courtroom.

The Prosecutor had still not seen the arresting party and, as though weary, he took off his lawyer's jacket and hung it on a brass hook in an alcove. Perhaps it was some involuntary noise that A. had made which caused the Prosecutor to turn.

The Prosecutor's face was red, and there were beads of sweat on his brow. He reached into the pocket of his hanging jacket for a handkerchief, and with this he mopped his face. He was shaking, as though he had been facing an ordeal himself. He looked cursorily at the three guards; his gaze rested on A. for a moment, and then he stared away down the corridor. But A.'s face must have prompted some degree of recognition in the man; the Prosecutor turned, and stared at A.

The prisoner was aware of the fact that the Prosecutor had aged. He saw his tiredness.

The Prosecutor stared at him, and then he raised his hand, finger pointing. His finger shook, as if he was recovering from some unknown emotional ordeal. "You! I recognise you!"

A. in turn stared at the heated face of the Prosecutor, but said nothing. He looked away.

"Bring him here!"

The guards forced A. to face the Prosecutor.

The Prosecutor walked towards the accused man; for a moment it seemed that a heavy weight was lifted from the Prosecutor's shoulders, for, wiping his hands on his crumpled handkerchief, he seemed almost willing to shake hands with A.; he extended one hand slightly, the fist half open. Instead of shaking A.'s hand, however, he grasped the sleeve of his coat.

A. smelled the sweaty smell of the Prosecutor; undoubtedly the man had been through some intense physical ordeal.

"When did you return to the city?"

"An hour ago."

The Prosecutor smiled a smile of relief. He shook his head, deprived of the power of speech for a second, but when he did speak it was with a subdued and hoarse voice, quite out of character, as far as A. could see, for he had only heard the man harangue and harass accused men and their witnesses. The Prosecutor's soft voice was at once filled with gladness and sorrow, and entirely unfeigned. "I admire you for the honour you have shown by your return." He released *A*.'s sleeve.

"What honour have I shown?"

"You have vindicated the honour of the city by appearing for sentence at the end of your trial."

"What trial was this? How could I have been tried?"

"Your absence made a difficulty but, as you know from your own early experiences in the city, you will see that the statutes conform because of a certain precedent."

A. looked at the Prosecutor and saw that, unmistakably, tears had formed in the man's eyes.

"It's a fine example," the Prosecutor was saying. "Believe me, this will be published." He looked up and down the stone-flagged corridor, aware that this was no place to talk in. He reached out to *A*.'s arm again, as if to lead him to some more private place – the corridor was no place to talk – but, on looking at his watch, he desisted. "Have you anything to say?"

"No."

"That, too, does you credit."

A. leaned forward, though his two arms were now pinioned by the guards. He made no attempt to shake off their grip. "So I have been tried in my absence?"

"Of course." The Prosecutor paused. "You must have undoubtedly known that a trial would take place; it was inevitable."

A. saw that the Prosecutor's mouth was beaded with flecks of spittle at the corners, as if the man had a moment before, been declaiming violent and accusatory oratory in the courtroom. "You have set us all an example," he said quietly.

"Why is that?"

"Because of your voluntary return at the end of your trial." The Prosecutor spoke as if saying a self-obvious thing. A moment later his self-certainty vanished and he stared at the young man before him. It was clear that a doubt was growing in his mind. "When you returned, what did you expect to find? Did you expect your crime to be forgotten? Or what? And, if you were in the least part of your mind aware of the precepts of this city, why did you return?"

"My return seems to have been inevitable."

The Prosecutor would have asked further questions, had not a figure appeared at the end of the corridor.

*

A figure appeared at the end of the corridor, walking briskly towards them. This figure, seen at first as a silhouette against the light that flowed from a high window, became a man. He was a young man, perhaps in his late twenties. He was of slightly above average height; he was taller than the Prosecutor, but he could not be called tall. His slimness emphasised his height. His dress was that of a city lawyer; his white shirt was clean and formal. His hair was slightly longer than was customary, and coarse and black, but already there were grey steaks in it. His face was narrow, but he had prominent cheekbones. He dismissed *A*. with a very cursory glance, but stood by the condemned man as he faced the Prosecutor. *A.*, in the proximity of this unknown young man, was aware of his unwitting closeness, and of the unmistakable male animality of the man.

When the newcomer spoke, his voice was deeper than might have been expected from so slim a man. "Excuse me, sir." He bowed slightly to the Prosecutor. At that moment it was easy to see, as it were behind him, his wife and children, his obligations and limits.

"What is it?" The Prosecutor's voice was mild; the young man was obviously a favoured protégé.

"Perhaps, sir, we ought to be sure that there is no mistake in identity." The tone of his voice, though by no means abject or even deferential, showed his position in the hierarchy of which he was a member.

"It's a good thought." The Prosecutor's words were studied.

As though by cue two of the guards began to strip *A.* One of them ripped his shirt to expose the faint birthmark above his left clavicle. The other lifted *A.*'s hand to show the scar on the anterior aspect of the left forearm. The Prosecutor watched this with some interest. He turned to the young man. "Is that enough proof?"

"Yes."

For a second *A.* caught this young man's glance. The condemned man expected to see official neutrality or impersonal hostility. He saw neither of these expressions; he saw only an indiscriminate pity.

*

The door was opened by one of the guards.

The death-cell was a small high-ceilinged chamber, without windows but brightly lit. For a second A., startled by what he saw, saw nothing but the hanging corpse with the hooded head; then he saw the rope, the executioner, the doctor, the governor, and a few more unrecognisable faces.

It was clear that the door had been opened prematurely. The several officials, on seeing the door open, ceased staring at the hanging corpse and stared instead at A.

The door was closed again. The young man with the greying hair looked at his watch; once he opened his mouth as if to speak to A., but he was unwilling or unable to say anything.

*

A. stood in the cell, on the wooden platform. He looked at the faces which stared at him; he was able to detect no judgement in them. He saw only pity.

The Prosecutor entered the room. "I had to come," he said, addressing nobody, but speaking aloud.

A. certainly felt no sense of honour. Yet, despite this, had he not known the eventual outcome? Had he not known that his journeying would end at the place of his origins? Otherwise, why had he risked violent death in his travels to die here?

The executioner approached him, holding the black hood. He raised his hands to pull the hood over A.'s head.

A. looked into each of the pitying faces. "Wait," he said.

The young man with greying hair looked at his watch. Perhaps his position in the hierarchy precluded his speaking, but he did speak, his voice following the echoes of *A.*'s appeal. "Perhaps –" He turned to the other men. "Has he made his confession?" His tone of voice suggested that he earnestly wished to prolong *A.*'s life.

The Prosecutor stared at the young man as though the latter had asked a foolish question. "He was absolved *in absentia*," he said.

*

The execution was conducted in accordance with the usual principles. Five men were present to witness the event; the Prosecutor, the Prosecutor's clerk, the governor, the doctor, and the executioner.

The execution over and the death certificate signed and the act officially recorded, the dead man's family would be permitted to take possession of the corpse and to bury it according to the procedures of the Church. If, as seemed likely in this case, the dead man had no family, the corpse would be buried at the expense of the city in a windswept and steeply inclining cemetery that lay up in the hills, near the railway.